COUNTRY GIRL

Edie hurried out, letting the screen door close softly behind her.

"Nice girl," she heard Jake say. "I think this is going to be an even better summer than I figured on."

Edie walked quickly to the truck, looking down at her old sweater and shabby jeans. She hadn't even bothered with makeup. But none of that seemed to matter to Jake.

Maybe this time would be different. *But don't get carried away,* she told herself sternly. *Don't get carried away, and you won't get hurt again.*

Country Girl

Melinda Pollowitz

BANTAM BOOKS
TORONTO · NEW YORK · LONDON · SYDNEY

RL 5, IL age 11 and up

COUNTRY GIRL
A Bantam Book / March 1983

Cover photo by Pat Hill.

ISBN 0-553-23287-8

Published simultaneously in the United States and Canada

*Bantam Books are published by Bantam Books, Inc. Its trademark,
consisting of the words "Bantam Books" and the portrayal of a
rooster, is Registered in U.S. Patent and Trademark Office and in
other countries. Marca Registrada. Bantam Books, Inc., 666 Fifth
Avenue, New York, New York 10103.*

PRINTED IN THE UNITED STATES OF AMERICA

O   0 9 8 7 6 5 4 3 2 1

Country Girl

Chapter One

Edie Edmunds left the counter in the middle of Book Bayou and went up the two steps into the children's department of the store. With Miss Harriet out for her usual lunch of grilled cheese sandwiches at Jesperson's, Edie could use this time to open the new shipment of books and arrange some of them in the window. It would be a good way to keep her mind off Sean.

Darn him.

I'll just keep busy, Edie told herself, *till I find out about Sean—and Liza—for sure.*

She smoothed her new yellow sundress and ran her fingers through her wavy golden-blond hair, flipping it under at the shoulders the way

1

she liked it. This side of the store had its own door to the sidewalk, and Edie looked over at the two boxes the mailman had stuck inside earlier. She hoisted one carton onto the window ledge and carefully slit the tape with her Exacto knife.

As she lifted out twelve copies of *The Ox-Cart Man*, Edie noticed Liza Melsheimer in front of the pizza place across the street. Liza was twirling the long, hand-painted belt on her tight khaki shorts. Edie glared at her for a moment. Then, returning her attention to the stack of books in front of her, she put aside a copy to take home for Becky. Miss Harriet was really nice about letting Edie borrow books to read to her little sister. "Take home anything you want," she would say. "Just read them with their jackets off so they won't look too worn out to sell later."

Edie marked the books off the invoice and decided it must have been in sixth grade when Liza started to become unbearable. That was the year Mrs. Melsheimer had started letting Liza wear makeup to school. Liza had been miles ahead of Edie ever since.

Liza's tan showed signs of careful work for mid-July. Her golden shoulders above her khaki halter top were unmarred by strap marks. Edie

2

picked up the second carton of books and tried to stop watching Liza sauntering back and forth along the sidewalk. She was probably meeting somebody for lunch. Sean? She hoped it wasn't Sean. She hoped so hard it hurt. If only what her best friend Julie said wasn't true—that Sean had taken Liza to the drive-in on Saturday night.

Not everybody can be as rich as Liza Melsheimer, Edie thought angrily. Not everybody could afford to lie around on the Petoskey beaches all summer. She knew it didn't do any good to feel jealous, but she couldn't help it.

It was sort of silly, though. She didn't really have any proof about Sean and Liza. Not yet. And anyway, Sean just couldn't go for Liza . . . could he? Not after those two dates with Edie. All right, so what if they hadn't exactly been honest-to-goodness *dates*? He had held her hand both times, hadn't he? Their first date was to get ice cream on the next to last day of school. And their second one was when he came into Book Bayou to pick up his mother's stationery and they ended up going out for fries and Cokes at lunchtime. That was already two weeks ago, but still there was the way he had looked at her when he said he'd have more free time after the tennis tournament. What did that mean? It meant more free time for Edie, didn't it? And he did say she had a cute smile; told her he loved her dimples. . . .

Since there weren't any customers in the store, Edie closed her eyes a minute to remember better. She could picture Sean Turcott striding the halls of the high school, tall and strong, like Launcelot. And for a while, just a while, Edie Edmunds had thought she could be his Guinevere. . . .

Please, not Liza Melsheimer, Edie thought. Liza had never helped him last year when he was editor of the school paper. Edie had typed copy and run it to the printer so Sean wouldn't be late for basketball practice. What had Liza ever done for him? Nothing.

Edie opened her eyes just as Sean's little yellow convertible flashed to a stop outside. There he sat, relaxed behind the wheel, his longish blond hair blown back from his handsome face. He was dressed for tennis, in a white terry top and white shorts. Edie watched him lean over to open the door for Liza.

Suddenly Edie looked at her yellow dress and slid the carton of books to the floor, crouching down, hiding herself. If Sean looked toward Book Bayou, would he guess? That Edie had bought her dress to match his car?

She could feel her eyes smarting with tears.

4

Maybe her sister Kate had been right about love all along. Maybe boys weren't worth the trouble they caused. Big sisters were right sometimes, weren't they?

Edie blinked back the tears so she could see to run her knife along the top seam of the carton. She yanked the flap back and looked inside. Mildred Ames's latest novel was on top. At least she'd have that much—a really good book to read after work.

Darn Liza, with her seventy-two hand-painted belts, Edie thought. *Sean must have lost his mind. And why did I have to tell Julie I was sure Sean was in love with me? All along, Julie said they weren't real dates. Just his way of thanking the slaves, Julie said. But he held my hand and looked at me like he was promising things. That wasn't fair.*

When Edie stood up, Sean and Liza were gone. She unpacked the rest of the new books, then crawled into the window to pull out the old ones.

All in all, it had not been a good morning. Aside from Sean and Liza, there had been the visit from the Lamoreaux sisters a little earlier in the day. What a pair they were! Miss Harriet had warned her there would be customers like

5

the Lamoreauxs, but Edie couldn't believe how bad these two really were.

"I can't imagine what could be keeping Harriet," Virginia Lamoreaux had kept saying over and over again. "She's never taken more than half an hour for lunch in all the years she's been in business. And it's not even noon. Are you positive she said she was just going over to Jesperson's?"

"That's where she always eats," Edie had said. "But she might have said something about an errand to run. I think she did."

"Why, surely that's what *you've* been hired for," Virginia said, her chocolate-colored fingernails beating a tattoo on the open Christmas card catalog in her lap. "Errands, I mean. I can't believe Harriet would leave a new person like you in charge of Book Bayou for so long."

"I'm not so new," Edie said, her blue eyes flashing.

"Well! You certainly were not working in here last summer," Virginia said.

Crystal, Virginia's twin, who was a plump version of Virginia, puffed into the book room from the other side of the store, fumbling with the lid of her hand-painted wooden bag. "Ginny, do let the child be. When you're quarrelsome, your voice carries for miles. Let's not wait for

Harriet anymore. She wasn't in Jesperson's a bit ago when we were having our lemon pie, so she must've gone off somewhere else."

"She'll be really sorry she missed you," Edie said. "I'll bet she had to get some special orders to the post office. You know how long those lines can be."

"Come, Ginny. Can't we just go on back out to Walloon Lake?" Crystal asked. "You can choose your Christmas cards some other day."

"If you'll exert yourself to think for a minute," Virginia said, "it wasn't Christmas cards we came for. It was those filthy books!" Virginia flung her arm toward the display of paperbacks across the room. "*Love's Raging Revival*, indeed!" She tightened the scarf knotted around the bun of gray hair at the nape of her neck and stood up. She and Crystal marched across the room.

"Smut," Virginia said. "Nobody back in Louisiana would ever believe Harriet stocks such trash."

"But they're selling really well," Edie said. "Everybody's reading them." *Maybe I ought to start reading a few myself. To find out how to keep Sean away from Liza.*

"Humph," grunted Virginia. "You can tell Harriet I am disappointed, *sorely* disappointed.

I can't imagine what our friends back home are going to think. Tell her we'll be in again first thing next Thursday."

"OK," Edie said, trying not to flinch at the finger Virginia was shaking in her face. "First thing."

"Why, look at that!" Crystal suddenly squealed. "Jeremy's found a parking space right out front. Isn't he a genius? Let's go now, Ginny."

Edie looked out the window at Jeremy, waiting patiently by the car. She wondered how on earth he'd managed to put up with chauffeuring the Lamoreaux sisters around for so many years.

As soon as the sisters were settled in the car, Edie hurried to the basement door opposite the cash register, opened it, and called down the stairwell, "All-ee, all-ee, in free, Miss Harriet! You can come up now."

Miss Harriet's curly gray head poked around the corner at the bottom of the staircase. "Are you certain? You actually watched them get into their car?" Her voice held just a trace of her native Baton Rouge drawl. So many years up north had turned her into just about as much of a Michigander as Edie was.

Edie grinned. "They're gone. But I think you're going to be in trouble with the folks back

8

home in Louisiana. Virginia's toes were curling over those romances."

"Is that what the old bat wanted this time?" Miss Harriet climbed the stairs, her hands full of back issues of *Publishers Weekly*. "At least I had a chance to catch up with some of these. I hope she wasn't too tough on you. I just wasn't up to taking on Virginia today. What'd you tell her?"

"That everybody was reading romances. She said she's coming in again next Thursday. Early."

"Well, we'll just lock up, if we see them coming in time." Miss Harriet took off her glasses and polished them on the hem of her olive-green cardigan. Her brown eyes sparkled with irritation. Then she took off the sweater and hung it on a hook by the wall telephone. "Last week it was Huck Finn she wanted off my shelves. It's *always* something. Coming up here every summer, telling me how to run my business."

"She *is* pretty awful," Edie agreed. "Listen, why don't you really go and have your lunch now?"

"I might as well, I guess." And with that, Miss Harriet had left, leaving Edie to worry about Sean and Liza.

Now Edie saw Miss Harriet jaywalking

through the heavy stream of summer traffic back to Book Bayou. She hurried to the basement for the small vacuum cleaner she used to rid the windows of dead flies. For a moment, Edie rested her cheek against the cold stones of the basement wall.

I won't be like those dead, dumb flies upstairs. Buzzing at the glass till it's too late. Too dumb to back off and try another way out. I'll just make something else matter, like Miss Harriet and my job at Book Bayou. At least, I still have that.

Edie grabbed the vacuum off the top of the refrigerator that Miss Harriet kept stocked with soft drinks, cashew nuts, port-wine cheese, and frozen M&M's for emergencies.

Darn Sean, she told herself, climbing back upstairs. *And darn Liza Melsheimer, too!*

Chapter Two

The sidewalks were still crowded with summer shoppers when Edie left Book Bayou at five-thirty. Miss Harriet was the only store owner on the street who refused to stay open late just because July had come and the town was full of tourists and resorters with money to spend. Edie couldn't have worked any later, anyway, not without a lot of trouble. She had to be on time to catch a ride home with her father or else find her own way out to the farm down fifteen long, dusty country miles. In September, when she turned sixteen, she'd have a driver's license. Not that it would make things much easier; not when her family didn't have anything extra sitting around in the driveway for her to drive.

Edie stood at the crosswalk, waiting for the WALK sign to flash on, feeling unhappy in the yellow sundress she'd been so happy to put on that morning. *Now I'll never wear it again,* she thought. *Not ever.*

Mr. Edmunds sold washing machines at the Sears store down the block, next door to the Holiday movie theater. Edie could see a group of people already milling around in front, waiting to buy tickets for the six o'clock show. *I'll die if Sean and Liza are in that movie line,* she thought. *I can't face them. Not with Liza so tan and me so pale from working inside all summer.*

Edie swung her Book Bayou shopping bag, trying to look nonchalant as she approached the theater.

Of course, Liza may be tan now, but she'll probably be all wrinkled and leathery in another ten, maybe fifteen, years. Then she'll have to stay out of the sun completely. By then, I'll be a famous journalist working on the New York Times, *and I'll just happen to pop into Petoskey right after I've covered the bullfights in Portugal, or some other sunny* place. *I'll have a sensible, toasty tan, and I'll walk right up to Sean's desk in Sean's father's bank where Sean is sure to end up one day, and he'll be swiveling in his swivel chair with his three-piece suit bunchy over his middle-aged spread. And I'll whip out my checkbook and I'll pay off the mortgage on the farm, just like that, and Sean won't be able to stop looking at my expensive beige outfit, or my legs. And he'll say, let's get some coffee, and right off, he'll admit how miserable he is being married to Liza Melsheimer, who's too wrinkled to go outside anymore. I'll just nod and pretend to feel sorry for him, and then I'll say I have to dash. And I'll just leave him sitting there in the booth, looking sad, and kicking himself for missing his chance all those years ago when we were kids.*

Sean and Liza weren't in the movie line. However, Edie's best friend, Julie Stevens, a tall, slender brunette, was just getting out of her father's car, her younger brother J.J. III behind her. Edie's father's old truck, parked a few spaces up the street, was still empty. *All right*, Edie thought, *I might as well get it over with now, while Dad still has a customer. I'll let Julie say I told you so, and then I can go home.*

"Hey, Edie!" Julie called, tossing her thick braid of hair over one shoulder. "Stay and see the show with us. Dad can drive you home later."

"I'd like to," Edie replied, "but I can't. I just wanted to tell you something." She sighed. "You were right about you-know-who and last Saturday night at the drive-in. He picked her up at the pizza place today. Actually, they're a nice-looking couple."

"You know you don't mean that," Julie said. "I was hoping it wouldn't turn out to be true, for your sake. I hope you're not going to have a long face for the rest of the summer."

J.J. began to look bored. "Go and buy the tickets and get in the popcorn line," Julie told him. "I'll meet you there." J.J. walked away, clutching the money.

"I'm not going to let Sean spoil my summer, don't worry. I'm not that much of a romantic idiot. I mean, maybe I did care for a while, but after all, until today I hadn't seen him for two entire weeks. I was probably beginning to outgrow him." Edie lowered her gaze. Her blond hair, falling over her face, veiled the hurt in her eyes.

"You'll never be a convincing liar," Julie

14

said. "Come on. Stay for the movie and cheer up."

"I can't. I promised Becky I'd take her to see this sometime, and I can't afford to see movies twice. Not on my budget."

"You and your budget. What have you bought all summer, except for that yellow dress? I'd burn it tonight, if I were you. Or you could invite me to sleep over on Saturday, and we could burn it together."

"You can sleep over," Edie said, "but I'd never burn a perfectly good dress. Mom would *kill* me if I wasted money like that." *But*, Edie thought, *she won't notice if I bury it in the back of my closet, forever.*

"Oh, here comes your dad," Julie said suddenly. "You go on home and have a good cry. I'll call you tomorrow."

"Who's going to cry?" Edie said. "Not me. Have fun at the movie." She ran to the truck and climbed into the front seat next to her father. The lines in his thin face seemed even deeper in the summertime. He looked tired.

"Bad day?" Edie asked. "Or just a busy one?"

John Edmunds rolled his eyes and pulled out into the stream of traffic. "Never saw such a summer," he said. "All this traffic downtown, and everybody and his brother needs a new washer and a new dryer all installed by tomorrow."

"We weren't busy till after lunch," Edie said. "But the Lamoreaux sisters were in this morning to tell Miss Harriet off again."

"Try finding a washing machine to suit those two if you want real fireworks," Mr. Edmunds said, giving her a half-smile.

He and Edie rode along in silence for a while, away from the busy downtown streets. The gas stations, the fast-food stops, and the traffic began to thin out and were replaced by trees, fields, and herds of cows grazing on long, sweet grass. Edie rolled her window down to let the wind off Lake Michigan blow through the truck.

Mr. Edmunds began to whistle and look more relaxed. "I hope your brother managed to get all those ripe berries picked today," he said. He turned left off the paved highway onto the narrow gravel road that roller-coasted all the way to the Edmundses' small dairy farm. At the top of the first hill, he turned and grinned at Edie.

"One thing I meant to tell you this morning, Edie . . ."

"What was that, Dad?"

"That you look mighty special in that new yellow dress. It lights up your face."

"Really? Thanks!" Edie said, trying to sound enthusiastic for her father. She rested her head against the window and thought about him. He cared so deeply for his family, and he worked so hard for them. Edie knew he hated these short-money times when he had to get a job downtown, letting Edie's mother and older brother Michael run the farm. He had to worry about taxes and vet bills and broken equipment, plus college money for Edie. She was the only one of the four Edmunds children who wanted to go to college. It was her dream. She saw herself reading in a big, university library. It was dark and snowy outside, but inside she was warm, and the fluorescent lights were so bright. . . .

She closed her eyes, trying to will Sean out of her mind. He was still there when her father bounced the truck up the uneven ruts of the gravel driveway and squealed to a stop by the front porch. But he was fading, just a little.

Ruby Edmunds pushed Edie's wavy golden hair away from her face and stroked it a moment. "You a bit down tonight?" she asked.

"You've been awfully quiet. Let me finish up these dishes so you and Kate can run Becky to the creek before dark."

"I've just got the pots left to go, Mom," Edie said. "And you've been up to your elbows in pickle juice all day."

Mrs. Edmunds edged Edie away from the sink with one hip. "Pickles I'm used to. Go on and have a run. I don't want you getting worn out with your job downtown and the housework around here."

Edie dried her hands on the raggedy denim cutoffs she'd changed into after work and pulled down the sleeves of her favorite old sweater. "OK. Maybe some exercise will perk me up."

"Perk you up from what, I'd like to know." Kate snapped her dish towel at Edie's rear end. "From your cushy job? Reading books all day long? I'll never get the smell of brine off my hands, after today."

"Come on, Kate. You know I don't get to read all day long."

Mrs. Edmunds tossed Kate a lemon off the windowsill. "Squeeze that over your hands. It'll take care of the brine. And next spring, remind your father not to get carried away when cucumber-planting time comes."

18

Mr. Edmunds grabbed up Kate's dish towel and grinned at his wife. "Same amount I put in every year. Besides, I don't notice anybody complaining when they're munching away on pickles all winter long. And another thing, seems to me I heard somebody around here say she wanted to stay home and help out."

"I seem to have heard the same thing." Mrs. Edmunds handed her husband a wet pan.

"All right," Kate said. "I guess making pickles is still better than working downtown in the summer. I hate all those rich people running around on their three-month vacations."

"You're just jealous," Edie said. "Come on, let's go if we're going. I think I saw Becky go under the snowball bush, chasing her ladybugs."

Edie stopped at the screen door to look back at her parents. Her mother's dark blond hair, streaked with silver, shone in the golden twilight coming through the window. She was smiling up at the thin man studiously wiping the corn pot dry. *That's what love looks like,* Edie thought. She let the screen door swing closed behind her with a whisper.

"So what's really eating you tonight?" Kate asked as they crossed the yard to the snowball bush. "If it's because you haven't heard from Sean again, just remember I told you not to count on anything there. He's a creep."

"I just had a hard day, that's all," Edie said. "Sean's not special, anyway. We just had fun together."

"Well, I'm glad to hear you say that, because he's cut from the same cloth as Steve Farrington, and don't you ever forget it. Even if Sean does live here year-round, he still has the money to act like a resorter, and he's looking for a rich girl, same as Steve was. If I were you, I'd stick with John Mason. Whatever happened to him? He was nice."

"I don't know," said Edie, remembering their few dates. "He was boring."

She parted the branches of the snowball bush, scattering white petals, and peered into the darkness. "Come on out, Beck, we're going to the creek." *And hurry, before Kate really gets going on Steve Farrington,* she thought. *Three straight summers of going steady, and then Steve dumps her. She's never gotten over it. And with her straight blond hair and light blue eyes, she could have anyone she wants. If only she'd give the guys a chance.*

A girl, with her hair in ponytails and very

dirty, bare feet, crawled out from under the bush on all fours. "I'm not finished catching my ladybugs," she said. "I've only got forty so far, and last night I had forty-six."

"Maybe they're hiding," Edie said. "Did you ever think maybe they don't exactly look forward to getting stuck in your shoebox night after night?"

"They know I always let them go as soon as everybody's counted. Maybe there'll be some in the hollyhocks."

Kate caught Becky by the belt on her jeans as she started for the hollyhocks. "Let them loose, Beck. If you don't come to the creek with us, Mom'll make you take a bath for sure. Just look at your feet."

Becky looked at her dusty feet and considered. Then she took the lid off her shoebox and dumped the ladybugs out on the snowball bush. "See you tomorrow, gang."

"Must be nice to be seven years old," Kate said as Becky ran ahead of them. "You make your bed, and you're through for the day. Now, tell me. Have you seen Sean again or not? What made you decide he's not so special all of a sudden?"

"Oh, I see him around. I think he's got a thing going with Liza Melsheimer."

"There's another spoiled brat."

"Kate, not everybody rich is rotten! I mean Liza definitely is, but not everybody. I'm going to catch up with Becky."

"Go ahead. I'm taking it easy."

Edie ran through the lengthening shadows, leaped the rail fence that separated the pasture from the yard, and grabbed Becky's hand. Their bare feet flashed over soft patches of mullein and twisted away from cow pies and thistles. Around them, Indian paintbrush, dotting the field, caught fire from the lowering sun. Edie bounced to a stop at the wire gate that led to the woods and waited for Kate to catch up. Becky sat astride the gate, sticking bits of purple clover into her blond ponytails.

Edie looked out at the hills in the distance, the dappled shadows in their hollows, the sky above streaked coral and gold. Around her stretched her father's fifty acres. *I feel so peaceful in the middle of all this space, like nothing can go wrong.*

"Edie? Do you know what goes 'oom-oom'?" Becky asked.

"Nothing I ever heard of. What?"

"A cow walking backward!" Becky screamed. "Don't you love it?"

"You bet," Edie said. "I love it." Then she swung the gate open for Kate and followed her through. Once among the trees, Edie felt better. If she could just feel like this all the time. . . .

Chapter Three

It was dark in the woods and already cool. Edie's feet sank into the damp compost of leaves and pine needles on the path. "Don't you love that cedar-chest smell in here?"

"I don't smell cedar chest. I smell leaf rot," Kate said.

"It smells spooky is what it smells," Becky said. "I hope that Gus Hartwick person won't come after us."

"He won't," Edie said. "We're on our own property."

"You know, I've only seen him five or six times in all the years we've been neighbors,"

Kate said. "Wouldn't you think he'd have to come out more often than that?"

"Dad says he's happy living on the squirrels he shoots," Edie said. "And he fishes in the creek, so I guess he doesn't need to come out very often, even for groceries."

"I bet he has to come out to buy Kool-Aid," Becky said, running past Edie and leaping down the creek bank to the water. "I think the next time he does, we should tell the police to come and get him."

"Silly," Edie said, following her into the creek. "Mr. Hartwick's not a criminal. He just got tired of living with people so close around him."

"I'll bet he murdered somebody once," Becky said, peering nervously at the top of the hill on the far side of the creek where Mr. Hartwick's property began.

Edie cupped her hands, filled them with water, and splashed Becky. "There's nothing to be scared of," she said. "Now get busy and clean your feet, Beck."

Becky scrubbed her feet into the sandy bottom. "If we walk in the water all the way to the back road, that ought to do it," she said.

"If our feet don't freeze off first," Edie said.

"You stay behind me so you don't stumble into any deep parts."

Kate got up from her seat on the creek bank and brushed leaves and twigs off her skirt. "You two are crazy. I'll take a hot bath anytime."

"Let's run, Edie," Becky said. "It's getting dark in here."

Edie took Becky's hand and led her through the rushing water. They ducked under a plank bridge that crossed the creek, then walked along the bank, passing the waterfall, which tumbled over a pile of granite boulders. "The creek gets deep past the waterfall," Edie said. "You remember that if you're ever out here by yourself."

"You tell me that practically every time," Becky said. "Where'd Kate go?"

Edie turned around to see Kate standing frozen against a cedar tree. She waved one hand weakly toward the opposite bank. "Hello, Mr. Hartwick," she said, but her voice was so low Edie could barely hear it over the noise of the waterfall.

Edie quickly looked to the bank and picked out the gaunt figure of a man from the surrounding gloom of the trees. He was wearing a heavy plaid jacket and a hunting cap, the expression on his face obscured by its brim and by the darkness under the pines. For just an

27

instant, he looked back at the girls, and then he vanished behind a screen of brush.

Becky clutched herself and shivered. "Did you see his big gun? Was he going to shoot us?"

"It was a fishing rod, I think," Kate said. "You and Edie both have too much imagination."

"Even if it was a gun," Edie said, "he wouldn't shoot at us. After all, he does know who we are."

"He didn't exactly say hello," Becky said.

"Hermits don't have to. We'd better start for home. Give me a hand up, Kate."

"He must get so lonesome," Kate said, reaching to pull Edie up the slippery bank. "Boy, he sure gave me some scare!"

"I bet we gave him one, too," Edie said.

"I'm going to have nightmares," Becky said.

"Beck, he's just a strange old man. He wouldn't hurt you." Edie swung Becky's arm as they walked through the trees to the blackberry clearing by the back road. "Let's cut over here and go home through the cows. That way you can tell Clemmie good night."

"Oh, good," Becky said. "Maybe I'll get there when she's starting to have her baby."

"Wait," Kate said, "I hear a car coming. Maybe it's Doctor Paul."

"It's probably just kids," Edie said.

The back road was a one-lane strip of dirt, an old logging trail cut through the trees years before. Doctor Paul, the young widowed vet whose property abutted the Edmundses', often used the road as a shortcut back to his place from the highway. But the high-school kids used it, too, driving to its end ten miles farther north at Weber Lake. Edie had heard plenty about the parties that went on out there, but she'd never been asked to any. Neither had Julie, for that matter.

"Did you know Doctor Paul came over today?" Kate said. "He came to look at Flossie's sore leg, and he said his nephew's just arrived from somewhere downstate to help out for the rest of the summer." Edie was glad to hear this, but she was surprised. Since Doctor Paul's wife Bonnie had died, he hadn't bothered to hire anybody at all to help out in the office.

"His nephew seems really nice," Kate said.

"I didn't even know he had a nephew," Edie said, poking at the nearest blackberry bush. "Remind me to come pick. These'll be ripe soon."

"His name's Jake Duncan," Kate said. "I'm glad Doctor Paul'll finally have some company."

When the car suddenly came into view, Becky squealed. "Isn't it beautiful? It's not Doctor Paul's crummy old jeep, that's for sure!"

Edie's heart thumped wildly as the yellow convertible streaked toward her. Sean had been home long enough to change to jeans and a sweatshirt. Liza was snuggled up next to him, her short, dark, curly hair contrasting with Sean's blond hair. Liza's long orange scarf snapped in the wind as she lifted her head from Sean's shoulder.

Sean didn't stop. He just slowed a little, grinning at Edie as he drove past, and Liza graced them with a tiny, bored wave. Then she said something to Sean and started laughing, and Sean laughed back. Finally the car was out of sight, swallowed up by trees.

And here I stand in my very worst old clothes, Edie thought miserably. *Like somebody's dumb stray cow. Nothing better to do with herself. Bet that's just what she said to make him laugh.*

"Were they movie stars?" Becky asked incredulously.

"Just a couple of bad actors," Kate said, putting one arm protectively around Edie's shoulders.

But Edie pulled away. "I told you he had a thing going with Liza. It's a free country, isn't it?"

Kate studied Edie for a moment. "Sure,"

30

she said. "Anyway, you've got more class in your little finger than Sean's got in his whole body. Let's go. There's rain coming. See those black clouds?"

The girls climbed the rail fence and started toward the herd of Holsteins clustered in the middle of the field. Becky ran ahead to find Clemmie and check on her unborn calf.

Edie trudged along after Kate, gazing at the sky, feeling as dark as it looked.

Ahead, Becky suddenly began screaming and ran toward the house. "Dad! Michael! Somebody! Call Doctor Paul! I can feel Clemmie's baby moving."

Edie looked up as a dark cloud scudded past the North Star. *I'll wish for college money from now on. Never again for love.* A bat zoomed over her head and disappeared in the magnolia tree. Edie ducked and followed Kate inside, where she found Becky already being tucked into bed upstairs. The new book was on her lap, and her extra pillow was propped against the headboard, ready for Edie to sit beside her and read to her.

Mr. Edmunds stooped to kiss Becky. "No worrying now. Clem'll have this baby all on her own as soon as she's ready. Rain coming or not."

"OK," Becky said. "I guess you're the expert." Then she added, "Daddy? I won't ever be afraid of Mr. Hartwick again, not after what you told me. Maybe I'll go visit him someday."

"Now hold on, Beck. Don't do that, I didn't mean to make you feel sorry for him. He doesn't want company barging in on him."

"What'd you tell her?" Edie asked.

"That Gus had sort of caved in after his wife died, and he took to the woods. You know the story. Only now Becky wants to adopt him. Promise you won't go bothering Mr. Hartwick, honey."

"I promise," Becky said, holding up crossed fingers. But Edie saw her other hand dart under the blanket so she could cross the fingers of her other hand without her father seeing.

"Night, Dad," Edie said as her father left the room. "Make sure I'm up in time in the morning."

"I will," Mr. Edmunds said. "Don't read too late."

The waxy pink of the magnolia blossoms gleamed and faded, faded and gleamed, as the scudding clouds covered and uncovered the moon. It was a beautiful night, spooky with rain coming.

New book in hand, Edie turned from the window and climbed into bed. She leaned back on her pillows, stretching the kinks out of her long legs. After just two chapters, Edie could tell the girl in the book wasn't going to have any problems with love. She was fifteen, too, but sensible, mature, and very intelligent—just like Edie was going to start being, tomorrow.

She got out of bed and dug the yellow dress out of the closet where she'd buried it under a pile of discarded stuffed bears. Carefully she put it on a hanger and smoothed out the wrinkles. *I'll wear it again one day, because Dad says it makes me look special. I'll wear it for him. I could even wear it just for me! I always did like yellow.*

Back in bed, with her eyes closed, Edie could see Sean and Liza laughing at her. A couple of tears slipped from her eyes. But when she thought about her family, and about Miss Harriet hiding in the basement from Virginia Lamoreaux, she laughed out loud. There was plenty of love around her. Enough for now.

Edie rolled over on her stomach and tried to make her mind blank. The first raindrops pinging gently on the old shingled roof overhead lulled her. As she drifted off, she thought only once more about Sean and Liza. That their party at Weber Lake must be getting rained out right now. Edie grinned and hoped the top of Sean's car would stick and not go up until Sean and Liza were both good and wet.

Chapter Four

Miss Harriet and Edie stood together by the front window of Book Bayou watching a river of water flow down Howard Street. A streak of lightning cracked the sky, thunder boomed, and the awnings over the sidewalk clanked against their metal posts as the wind wrenched at them.

"I think I better pull those things in now," Edie said, grabbing her slicker off the hook behind the counter.

Miss Harriet took down her raincoat and belted it around her. "I'll pull them in. I can't have you getting sizzled by lightning."

"And I don't want to watch you blow away."

Edie tied her hood under her chin and yanked the front door open.

"So we'll each do one awning," Miss Harriet said. "I'll get the far one." She and Edie waded through ankle-deep water, their raincoats flapping around their legs, rain blowing up their sleeves as they cranked in the heavy canvas. They were dripping by the time they fought their way back inside.

"I'll go downstairs and get some towels," Edie said, hanging up first her slicker, then Miss Harriet's raincoat.

"I'll go down with you. Let's kick off our shoes, and I'll make some hot chocolate. A little rain's good for business, but nobody in his right mind will be out in this."

Edie looked out the window. The pizza place across the street had the CLOSED sign flipped over the door. It looked abandoned and bleak in the rain. She shivered and followed Miss Harriet downstairs.

She and Miss Harriet toweled off quickly, and Miss Harriet made hot chocolate on the hot plate. She poured the hot chocolate into mugs and handed one to Edie. "Let's drink these while we keep an eye on this storm," she said, heading for the stairs.

Edie settled into one of the easy chairs by

the fireplace. Wind and rain battered the windows, and lightning lit the street. The fluorescent lights in the ceiling began to flicker and finally went dark. "I was waiting for that," Miss Harriet said. "I wonder where I put that silly flashlight?"

"I think it's under the cash register." Edie crossed the room in her stockinged feet and found the big red flashlight. "Here we go." She switched it on.

"At least it has batteries for once. Now, call your dad and see if he's ready to give up and go home. If he's not, I'll drive you out myself."

"Oh, it's much too far, Miss Harriet. I can just wait at Sears till he's ready." Edie dialed Sears by the light of the flashlight and spoke briefly to her father. "He's been itching to get home for hours," she said after she hung up. "They don't have any lights, either. And Dad can't stand a storm unless he's home putting the cows to bed himself. He'll be right over."

Edie carried her sopping moccasins to the front door. "Can you get home OK?"

"Takes more than a little rain to daunt a tough old bird like me," Miss Harriet said. "Don't give me a second thought. My car's right outside."

A few minutes later Mr. Edmunds's truck

eased to a stop in front of Book Bayou, water streaming past the tires. "Be careful," Edie said. "See you tomorrow."

"Not if it's still doing this. See what the weather's like."

"I'll call you first thing in the morning."

"Go, go," Miss Harriet said. "Before your dad pops a cork."

Edie splashed through the water to the truck, hunching her shoulders against the rain. Mr. Edmunds's face was grim in the light from the dashboard. "Creek'll be up. The barnyard's probably already under water."

"Don't worry, Dad. Michael knows what to do."

"We'll see."

The ride to the farm was slow and scary. Mr. Edmunds had to concentrate hard to keep the truck from sliding off the road. Edie kept quiet, knowing he would worry all the way, no matter what she said.

"We should've gone home hours ago."

"It would've been fine with Miss Harriet. She said not to come in tomorrow if it's still storming."

"Good. I hope Sears feels the same way, because I'll have one heck of a mess to clean up in the morning."

Someday I'll be earning all the money we need, thought Edie, *and Dad can stay on the farm for the rest of his life. Never again be stuck downtown working at a job he hates during a big storm.*

Mr. Edmunds drove straight to the barn and dashed out into the rain. Edie turned off the headlights and followed him. Lanterns hung on hooks around the upstairs hayloft, and several more lighted the stairway down to the dairy floor. Edie's brother had dropped the large curtain of cowhide over the doorway to the barnyard to keep out the wind. Sandbags blocked all the cracks along the width of the barn.

Michael, dripping in oilskins, was pushing the cows into their individual stanchions, wiping each cow dry with pieces of old sheets. A young man with frizzy, rusty-brown curls smiled at Edie as she came down the steps. His beard was beaded with drops of rain and was almost as frizzy as his hair.

"Doctor Paul sent Jake over to see if we needed help," Michael said. "All the cows are in, Dad, except for Clemmie. She wasn't with the others in the pasture. We were just going back out to look for her."

"I can't afford to lose Clemmie, or her calf,"

Mr. Edmunds said. "We've got to find her. Listen, whatever you do, don't let Becky know it's Clemmie who's missing. Somebody hitch the stoneboat to the tractor. I'll go check in with your mother, and then I'll drive the lane."

"I hate to say this, but Becky was down here helping out," Jake said. "She already knows about Clemmie."

"She said she was going up to the house to get Mom to call you downtown," Michael said.

"Oh, boy!" Edie groaned. She took the steps two at a time and flew up the path to the house.

"What's wrong?" Mrs. Edmunds cried as Edie banged into the kitchen, startling her mother and Kate, who were bent over the antique wood stove, trying to light a fire. "I'm not surprised Dad hauled you home early, but you're white as a sheet."

"It's Becky." Edie stood on the doormat, trying not to make puddles on the floor. "Is she up here with you?"

"She's in the barn with the boys," Kate said.

"No, she isn't. We've already been to the barn. Clemmie's missing, and Michael thought Becky came up here to tell you."

"I'll check her room. Maybe she slipped by

40

us in the dark." Kate kicked off her clogs and ran up the steps.

Mrs. Edmunds was already getting into her slicker and high boots. "She's gone after that cow for sure." She stepped onto the back porch as Mr. Edmunds drove up in the truck. "Don't get out, John!" Mrs. Edmunds called against the wind. "Becky's not in the house either. We've got to find her."

Kate banged open the window at the end of the upstairs hall. "She's not anywhere up here," she hollered down. "I'll wait in the house in case she comes back on her own."

Edie jumped into the front seat of the truck beside her mother. "I just can't believe she'd go out with all the lightning. She hates storms."

"She'd go through fire for Clemmie," Mrs. Edmunds said. "Thank goodness she was wearing her slicker."

"Crazy kid," Mr. Edmunds said. "As if I didn't have enough to worry about right now." He stopped at the barnyard gate long enough for Edie to hop out and swing it open. She barely had time to close the truck door again before Mr. Edmunds lurched off up the muddy lane. Michael roared out of the barn on the tractor, Jake riding the stoneboat attached behind. "The cows were in this pasture today,"

Mr. Edmunds said, waving to the field on the left of the lane. "Watch for a break in the fence. Find Clemmie and we'll find Becky, too."

Edie was the first to spot the break. "There. Clemmie's probably gone into the woods." A section of fence leaned askew, its broken rail splintered. "But maybe Becky hasn't found the break yet. Maybe she's still someplace in the pasture."

"All right," Mrs. Edmunds said, looking at the tractor, which had caught up with them. "Only the tractor can make it through the woods, so I'll stay here with the truck. I'll leave the headlights on and start searching the field."

"If she's out there, she'll come to the lights," Mr. Edmunds said. "Now don't get too far away." He gave his wife a quick hug, then jumped on the tractor hitch while Edie sat down on the stoneboat with Jake. Edie tightened the hood of her slicker.

"Get that look off your face," Michael yelled to her, his words almost lost in the wind. "Becky's a tough little kid. We'll find her OK."

Edie squinted her eyes against the rain and tried to see into each clump of trees. The stoneboat bounced clumsily over dislodged tree roots and clumps of dirt. Once Edie was thrown against Jake, but she was too worried to smile at him as he steadied her. Michael stopped the tractor along the bank of the creek. The roar of water was deafening as the noise of the tractor's engine faded away. "No wonder everything at home's flooded out," Edie said. "Look how high the creek is. I hope Becky isn't wandering around out here."

The creek was already overflowing its banks in several places, and the current was swift, tumbling the muddy water downstream.

"Becky! Becky!" Edie called. "Answer me." Her voice was barely audible above the thunder of the creek.

"You're wasting your breath," Mr. Edmunds said. "She won't hear you. You two go have a look down by the falls. Mike and I'll go the other way." Mr. Edmunds took two axes out of the toolbox under the tractor seat and handed one to Jake. "In case she's stuck under a tree."

"Oh, Daddy, don't say that!" Edie wailed, but no one paid any attention to her. Shouting every few steps for Becky, she followed Jake through the dripping trees beside the raging creek.

The falls were louder than anything Edie had heard before, and her mouth felt dry from fear. Then, on the other side of the creek, Edie thought she saw a figure stooping over the tumbling water. She wiped her eyes and looked again. It was a man, Mr. Hartwick, his sodden plaid jacket dragging at his thighs. He picked something up in his arms, a bundle of yellow. Wet hair hung over the crook of his elbow. Becky's hair!

"That has to be her," Jake said. "Who's the old man?"

"It's Mr. Hartwick," Edie said quickly.

"Mr. Hartwick, we're here!" Jake shouted. "We're over here! Is Becky all right?"

Mr. Hartwick didn't turn around. He climbed the bank and vanished into the trees. "We'll have to go across," Jake said.

"Let's check the bridge," Edie said. They ran around the bend in the creek, ducking under branches. The bridge was already mostly under water. But it held Jake's weight as he stepped gingerly onto it, grasping the handrail tightly. Once he was across, Edie followed, cautiously moving one foot at a time. The bridge vibrated in the wind, and Edie forced herself not to look into the heaving water.

"Just take it slow," Jake said. "You're nearly there."

A few moments later Edie was safely on the far side of the creek, too. "Good old bridge," she said. "But I'll bet it won't hold much longer. Let's hurry. That crazy old man's got Becky."

Jake held back the wet branches of a cedar so Edie could get past him along the path.

"I'll bet this trail leads right to his front door," Edie said.

Wet leaves slapped against their faces as they pushed their way down the narrow trail, forcing them to walk slowly. At last Mr. Hartwick's cabin came into view a few hundred feet away, set up high on a rise, facing the creek.

Edie raced across the clearing in front of the cabin and pounded on the door. Mr. Hartwick opened it, a candle stuck onto a tin pie plate in his hand.

"We saw you pull Becky from the creek," she said. "We hollered, but you didn't hear us. Is she OK?"

There was no smile on Mr. Hartwick's long, narrow face. "Sorry," he said. "I'm deaf as a post. She's a mite damp, but no real damage was done. Just got a whack on the head."

Edie ran to Becky, where she sat wrapped in blankets in a chair drawn close to the fire. Mr. Hartwick had wrapped a towel around her neck. Now he handed her a mug of hot chocolate as Edie touched the bruise on her forehead. "I smashed into a rock," Becky said, her eyes filling with tears. "I thought I heard Clemmie by the creek, and then I fell in."

"You're just lucky Mr. Hartwick was around to pull you out," Edie said. "You scared everybody half to death."

"I know," Becky said. "I'm sorry. I almost drownded."

"I did hear a cow carrying on," Mr. Hartwick said. "Or at least I thought I did. That's why I came out. Thought one of yours had managed to cross the creek."

"The cow's about to calve," Jake said. "She's probably hidden some place to have her baby."

Becky leaped up and threw off her blankets. "I knew I heard her! Let's go look some more."

Edie pulled Becky back into the chair, taking her on her lap and pulling the blankets over them both. "You're not going anywhere!" she said. "You've caused enough excitement for one night."

"How are we going to get back?" Jake asked suddenly. "The bridge'll be gone by now."

"I can drive you back the long way," Mr. Hartwick said, shrugging into his soggy jacket. "But let's let Becky dry out. Tell me where you left the others. I'll go tell them Becky is all right.

You three dry off and finish up the cocoa I made."

"I said all along Mr. Hartwick was a perfectly nice person," Becky said as soon as he started his old Chevy outside. "And don't you love his house?"

Edie looked around the one-room cabin. Against one wall was a little cot, and across from the cot was a wood-burning stove. Pots and pans, their bottoms winking in the firelight, hung on the wall.

All the other walls held shelves running from floor to ceiling, packed solidly with books. Old books, Edie noticed, with real leather covers. Hundreds and hundreds of books.

"Do you think he likes to read?" Becky asked.

"I'd say it was a possibility," Edie said. "I've never seen so many books crammed into one tiny room."

Edie watched Jake poking at the fire, making sparks fly. "I'll put some more wood on," he said. "Maybe this old guy's a retired professor or something."

"I never heard anything about that," Edie said. "I bet he'd just rather read than talk to people. He's sort of a hermit." *Funny that he never comes into Book Bayou. I'll ask Miss*

47

Harriet how come, first thing tomorrow. Mr. Hartwick could be the best customer we ever had.

"I sure hope somebody finds my cow," Becky said. Edie pulled her sister's wet hair off her face and leaned over to kiss her cheek. Jake was still crouching by the fire, rubbing his curls with both hands, trying to dry his hair. Edie watched him, noticing how brown his eyes were, with funny yellow lights in them when he smiled.

He stood up then and poured mugs of cocoa for Edie and himself.

"To the storm," he said solemnly, handing Edie her cup. The lights in his eyes danced.

"To when it's over, you mean," Edie added. *That must be what he meant to say. Unless . . . Did he say it because that's when he met me? Could that be?*

Jake stared at Edie a moment longer, then pulled a stool closer to her chair, and they settled down to wait, watching the firelight.

Chapter Five

"Yes. The power's still off out here, too," Edie said, holding the receiver closer to her ear to hear Miss Harriet over the static. "We're lucky we still have the phone. Dad would rather not bring me into town today. He's not going to Sears. He's got to stay here and move sandbags."

"I don't really think there's any sense opening up," Miss Harriet said. "I can't sell many books with only one flashlight. That lightning got the main power plant, and nobody'll have electricity till tomorrow."

"Nobody will be open in that case," said Edie. "Miss Harriet, I've been wondering if you've ever met Gus Hartwick, the man I told you about who rescued Becky?"

"Hmmff," Miss Harriet muttered. "I know him, all right."

"Well, anyway, he's some kind of incredible reader. His house is practically built out of books. How come he never buys any books from us?"

"I don't know. Maybe he hasn't got any money. Besides, you said yourself he hardly ever comes out of the woods. There's no accounting for hermits."

"Dad says he has plenty of money stashed away. I'm going to work on him. He'd be a terrific customer."

"You just leave Gus be. He's probably too old and creaky for Book Bayou now, anyway. Isn't he?"

"Well, he is kind of on the old side, Miss Harriet, but he didn't seem creaky yesterday. He's not a mess or anything like that."

"Hmmff," Miss Harriet said again. "Might be kind of interesting to see for myself, I suppose. But don't you tell him it was my idea!"

"I don't see why not, but I won't if you don't want me to. I'll see you Monday morning."

"Right-o," Miss Harriet said, then hung up.

Edie stared at the phone for a minute and

then hurried across the kitchen toward the laundry room. Mrs. Edmunds was throwing a second load of mud-streaked clothes into the washer. "Mom? Do you know if anything was ever going on between Gus Hartwick and Miss Harriet? Anything like a romance, I mean?"

"Oh, I doubt that, Edie. Gus got married late in life, but he was never the sort to chase after other women. Why? Do you think there was something going on?"

"I don't know. Miss Harriet sounded sort of weird when I mentioned his name, that's all. Maybe they had something going before Gus got married?"

"Could be, I guess. But as far as I know, Miss Harriet's never been interested in anything but her store."

"Well, she was young once. How old was she when she moved to town?"

"Good Lord, Edie! Ask Miss Harriet. Are you going to need a ride to work today?"

"No, Miss Harriet doesn't want to open up without lights. Is it still OK for Julie to sleep over tonight? I told her I'd call her back."

"As long as her folks can get her out here. She could stay till Monday morning when you and Dad go back to town, if she wants. She can help clean up the mess."

"She won't mind."

"Tell Julie not to come till suppertime, though," Mrs. Edmunds said. "I need you to run errands for me today. I want you to take some pickles and jelly over to Mr. Hartwick's. And you'll need to stop at Doctor Paul's. Dad needs formula for Clemmie's calves. Kate said she wasn't up to errands today, for some mysterious reason. You will drive slowly, won't you?"

"Mom, I've been driving that truck since I was thirteen. I'll stay on the back roads, I promise. Is Becky still in the barn?"

"Are you kidding? Clemmie's twins really knocked that child out. And she's beside herself that Clemmie doesn't have milk coming yet. She's got a baby bottle in each hand."

Edie looked out the window at the swampy yard littered with sodden heaps of leaves. "The rain's finally slowing down. I'll leave for Mr. Hartwick's in a little while."

"Be sure to wear your boots."

"I'll call Julie and help you fold the stuff in the dryer first."

"I was hoping somebody would say that," Mrs. Edmunds said.

Cautiously, Edie eased the truck down the muddy lane through the woods. She could see smoke from Mr. Hartwick's chimney rising into the gray sky and a corner of the roof of his cabin. *I'll be real polite and thank him for rescuing Becky, then convince him to come check out Book Bayou.*

Mr. Hartwick answered Edie's knock immediately. She held out the basket of food. "We just wanted you to have these things. To say thank you again for yesterday."

"Been thanked enough," Mr. Hartwick said. "But I'll enjoy this. Did you find your cow then?"

"Finally. Michael located her holed up way down the creek, by that bunch of white pine stumps. She had twins, but she can't nurse them herself yet."

"Becky'll be pleased to help out, I'd guess," Mr. Hartwick said with a little smile.

Edie hesitated at the door. "I—I wanted to ask about your books. Have you read every single one?"

"It's likely."

"Do you ever buy new ones? I'm working at Book Bayou this summer, for Miss Harriet, and I thought you might want to stop in one day and see what we have. Miss Harriet buys lots of unusual books."

"Miss Harriet, huh? Hmmff!" Mr. Hartwick said. "That old girl still alive?"

"She's only about sixty-five or so!"

"She's seventy if she's a day. But don't you tell her I'm the one who said so!"

"Come see for yourself someday. Will you?"

"Don't need a book just yet."

"Well, when you run out, we'll find you something good."

"I'll think on it. Well, there's work to do."

"Right. And I should've been at Doctor Paul's long ago. Thanks again, Mr. Hartwick." Edie flashed her biggest smile, dimples and all.

"Been thanked enough," Mr. Hartwick said, shoving the door shut with one knee, his hands full of pickles and jelly.

Edie drove on past Doctor Paul's house and pulled up beside the hospital at the bottom of the yard. As she stepped from the truck, Oscar, Doctor Paul's orange cat, streaked out the hospital doorway, yowling, and raced around the house toward the back. Jake, dressed in a green scrub suit, came running out after the cat. His hair was a high, wide mass of curls, and his beard was still frizzy from the rain. He flipped his hand in greeting as he charged past Edie. A long, bleeding scratch ran along his left arm. "Got to catch that stupid cat!" he hollered back over his shoulder. "It's important!"

Doctor Paul, a tall, kind-looking man in his mid-thirties, came to the doorway. He, too, was wearing a scrub suit. "Oh, hi, Edie. I guess you met my nephew, Jake Duncan, last night, didn't you? The hairy guy behind the cat?"

"Yes, he was a big help. Why's he chasing Oscar, anyway?"

"One of my patients needs a transfusion, and Oscar is the unwilling blood donor. He saw the stuff come out of the cupboard and took off. Look, why don't you go help Jake, and I'll get that formula loaded into your truck."

"I guess I'd better," Edie said. "Jake looked like he was way behind." She ran around the house and spotted Jake running toward a fence. She saw the cat streak under it. Passing Jake, Edie flopped over the top rail, catching her breath, looking for the cat. She spotted Oscar crouching in the high grass and slowly crept toward him. She was just a yard away when Oscar noticed her. Edie expected him to run again, but he just looked her up and down with his big round eyes. Edie leaned down and scooped him up. Oscar tucked his head into the hollow of Edie's throat and began to purr.

"Poor baby," Edie crooned. "Poor old Oscar."

Jake had panted up to Edie, and his face was bright red. "Sure," he gasped, "for you, he's just a harmless pussycat. Look how he ripped up my arm."

"Put a little iodine on it," Edie said. "I guess Oscar thought I wouldn't turn him in. But I guess we have to."

"Don't worry about him. He won't feel a thing. I'll fix him a special supper tonight to make up for it all. If he promises not to touch my one good arm."

"He's purring. I suppose that's a promise," Edie said. "I think you can trust him."

"About as far as a mountain lion," Jake said. "How come you run so fast, anyway? You must be one of those jog-seven-miles-a-day types."

Edie buried her face in Oscar's fur. "Don't be silly. I just have long legs."

Jake looked down at Edie's legs and let his eyes travel slowly all the way back to her face. "Nice legs, too," he said.

"Oh, sure. Especially in these high-style rubber boots."

"I'd've had mine on, too, if Oscar had informed me he was going to be so sensitive."

"Oh, just toss your sneakers in the washer," Edie said "The mud'll come right out."

Jake gave her a funny little grin as he

opened the door to the hospital for her. Edie brushed past him, whispering to Oscar.

Doctor Paul came into the room. "Good! At last, the prodigal cat has returned. Want to stay and watch, Edie?"

"No! Not me! I've got to get the formula back right away." Edie handed Oscar to Jake and backed out of the waiting room.

"Tell your dad I'll stop by tomorrow and have a look at Clem," Doctor Paul said, heading toward the operating room.

Edie hurried through the waiting room, letting the screen door close behind her.

"Cute kid," she heard Jake say to Doctor Paul. "I think this is going to be an even better summer than I figured on."

Edie walked quickly to the truck, looking down at her old red sweater, her shabby cut-offs, and the mud-splattered boots. She hadn't even bothered with lip gloss. But none of it seemed to matter to Jake.

Just don't get carried away again, she told herself sternly. *"Cute kid" could mean just that. Plain, old, everyday cute kid.* She wondered how old Jake was. Old enough for college, probably, with that beard, and Edie wasn't even sixteen yet. Still, he did say she had nice legs. And last night at Mr. Hartwick's he had made that strange toast, "to the storm." *Julie'll say none of it means a thing.*

Then Edie remembered the way Jake's eyes had lingered on her legs and traveled up to her face. A spurt of glee gripped her, and she laughed out loud inside the cab of the old truck. *This time's going to be different. No matter what Julie says.*

Chapter Six

"Some guys are born flirts," Julie said pointedly. "Just like some girls."

"That's basic," Edie said. "I have a brother, remember? But should I take Jake's compliments seriously or pretend they never happened or what?"

Julie peered at Edie's long, slim legs stretched out along her bed. "You do have nice legs," she said. "But why can't you ever just wait and see what happens? You turn that imagination of yours loose and get all worked up over nothing. Maybe Jake was just being friendly."

"It's only that I loved that special feeling I

got when Sean was around. Now he's gone. What if I never feel that way again?"

"Honestly, Edie! You haven't been the same since you read *Rebecca* last year. Real life just isn't all that romantic. Besides, you're only fifteen. Why are you worrying so much?"

"I don't know."

"Love's young dream is a lie," Julie said.

"But what about Dave? Don't you ever feel—special—with Dave?"

Julie unbraided her dark hair and let it fall gently over her shoulders. "Just when am I supposed to feel special? When he's bumped my nose for the fiftieth time with one of his lightning-fast good-night kisses? Or when he's calling to ask me if I want to go to the stock-car races with him?"

"That's mean," Edie said. "You're just not in love yet. Or else you need to find somebody you haven't hung around with for the past five years. Besides, you never have to worry about who's taking you to special stuff at school. Like the junior prom next spring."

Julie shrugged. "Are you worried about that already? What about John? You've been out with him. And remember Kurt Henderson from freshman year? You dated him for a while. Honestly, Edie, you act like there are no available guys around, and it's just not true."

"What would you do if somebody devastating asked you to go with him? Would you still go with Dave?" Edie asked, ignoring Julie's comments. The last thing she needed was a pep talk. She preferred to dream; to wonder and dream.

"Nobody devastating even goes to our school," Julie said dryly.

"Maybe somebody new and devastating will move to town. Or maybe somebody old will turn devastating over the summer. Don't you ever think ahead?"

Julie slid under her covers and punched up her pillow. "Your problem is you think too much. I'll bet you were already counting on going to the prom with Sean, weren't you? I'll bet you even had your outfit all figured out! Didn't you? C'mon, admit it!"

Edie pulled her nightgown over her head. "What if I did? I never could've afforded a dress like the one I wanted anyway."

"I hope you're not going to get all bent out of shape over the prom when it's only July. Please spare me. To be honest, I don't care if I never get to a prom, ever, in my whole life."

"It's not the prom! It's the—the *zing* I'm after. The way I felt when Sean was around."

"Oh, honestly," Julie said.

"I'll find somebody devastating," Edie said staunchly. "You wait and see. There are more interesting boys around than John and Kurt. Come on, let's go to sleep. Doctor Paul's coming tomorrow and—"

"And maybe Jake will come along, and you want to lie in the dark and plan romantic conversations, just in case."

"Right," Edie said. "Or at least figure out how to get the zing back. I know you're going to like Jake, Julie. He's not the least bit like Sean."

"I'm glad my mother said I could stay the whole weekend. I have to help keep your feet somewhere near the ground."

"What I can't figure out is how I ever got a best friend with absolutely no imagination at all," Edie said.

"Just be glad you did," Julie said. "Go ahead, go on and trance out. Don't mind me."

Sunday morning was sunny, brilliantly sunny. The sky was a deep blue, and a fresh breeze carried the scent of just-rained-on grass. In the backyard, Edie, Julie, and Michael were raking up the debris when Doctor Paul's jeep went down the drive to the barn.

Edie leaned her rake against a tree, tucked her lavender T-shirt into her jeans, and quickly ran her fingers through her hair. She watched Jake climb down from the driver's seat. "I think we'll take a break for a minute, Michael," Edie said.

"Well, hurry back," Michael said, as Edie and Julie made a dash for the barn. "The power's back on, and we want to watch the game at one. All this junk has to be carted away by then."

"Edie and I can finish up," Julie called over her shoulder. "We don't care about the game."

In the barn Doctor Paul was talking to Mr. Edmunds in Clemmie's box stall. Jake was kneeling in the straw beside Becky, cradling a calf across his thighs, and Kate was busy sweeping fresh straw into the cows' stalls.

Edie smiled at Jake as he looked up at her. Even in the dim light of the stall, his brown eyes sparkled. "This is Julie Stevens, Jake," Edie said. "Julie, Jake Duncan."

Jake nodded at Julie, but he flashed a smile at Edie.

Doctor Paul patted Clemmie on one huge black-and-white flank and leaned over to ruffle

Becky's hair. "I'm afraid you're out of a job now, young lady," he said. "But you got these babies off to a fine start."

"Now maybe she'll come up to the house long enough for a bath," Kate said. "How about it, Beck?"

"I might," Becky said. "After I'm sure Clemmie's doing this right. And after I brush them. And after I get them down for their naps. I might take a minute then."

"Mother's work is never done, huh?" Jake said.

"Hardly ever." Becky sighed.

Edie laughed, then walked out of the barn with the others. They emerged into the bright sunshine, and Doctor Paul slid behind the wheel of the jeep. "I've got a stack of paperwork to get to this afternoon," he said. "But I intend to watch that ball game while I'm at it."

Mr. Edmunds put a hand on Jake's arm. "How about if Jake stays for lunch with us? He can watch the game here. That way we can say thanks for helping us out with the cows in the storm. We just have to get that brush pile cleared away first."

Edie held her breath.

"I'd like to," Jake said. "I'd rather clear brush

than get stuck with my half of Uncle Paul's bookkeeping."

"Can't your papers wait, Doctor Paul?" Kate said. "It'd be nice if you could stay, too."

Doctor Paul patted Kate's hand where it rested on the door of the jeep. "That'd be great, but I'm too far behind as it is. Give me a rain check?"

"Anytime," Kate said.

"Don't forget it's your night to cook, Jake," Doctor Paul said. He turned to Mr. Edmunds. "I'm getting spoiled. I can cook simple things, but Jake makes real gourmet meals."

Mr. Edmunds chuckled. "Michael will get him back in plenty of time."

"We'd better go rake," Julie said as the jeep backed up the driveway. "Michael's looking cranky."

"Well, Jake," Kate said, "I'm glad you'll be staying for lunch. I'll go get it started."

"My pleasure," Jake said, smiling at Kate. Then he turned to Edie. "How old is Kate?" Jake asked.

"She's twenty," Edie said, slightly puzzled. "Michael's twenty-two. Julie and I are sixteen."

"Give or take a few months," Julie said. "How old are you?"

"Eighteen," Jake said. He frowned at Edie. "I would've guessed you were older."

"Nope," Edie said. "Afraid not." *Darn. He thinks I'm a baby.*

"What are you going to make for dinner tonight, Jake?" Julie asked, trying to signal Edie to loosen up the hurt look on her face. "I never knew a real chef before."

"I'm planning Chinese something-or-other," Jake said. "It's made out of whatever happens to be hanging out in the refrigerator."

Edie swallowed hard so her voice wouldn't squeak. "I could pick some green peppers to put in," she said. "They're just ripe."

"Great," Jake said, smiling at her again. Then he walked over to Michael. "Put me where you want me," he said.

"Well, the raking's done," Michael said, "without much help from certain people around here, I might add. But we still have to load up the wagon. Why don't you get up there, and the rest of us will toss the stuff up to you?"

"Sure," Jake said.

Edie went over to the pile of debris and dragged a tree limb to the wagon.

"Heave ho!" Jake said. "Swing it up easy." The branch sailed smoothly up to the wagon. "Hang on, Edie," Jake called as she started back

66

to the pile of debris. "You've got something in your hair." He reached over and brushed away a few leaves.

Julie was ready for Edie. "That was not a proposal of marriage, you know," she whispered. "That was just a simple 'brush-the-leaves-out-of-the-kid's-hair.' He would've done it for any-body."

Edie gathered up a load of small branches and glared at Julie. "Shut up. He'll hear you! Did he get all the leaves out?"

"You look fine," Julie said. "Quit worrying, will you? Just for a change?"

"I like how his beard waggles sideways when he smiles," Edie said, helping Kate pile club sandwiches on a tray.

"The smile's all right," Julie said, "but the beard's gross."

Edie carried the tray into the living room, where the boys and Mr. and Mrs. Edmunds were gathered around the television set. Jake took a sandwich from Edie's tray, nodded his thanks, and went right on talking to Michael. But when Kate came in with potato salad, he tasted it and said, "This is terrific. Secret recipe?"

"Don't be silly," Kate said. "I'll give it to you."

"Jake likes Kate," Edie whispered to Julie when they were safely back in the kitchen. "And she's two years older than he is. It's not fair."

"When'd you decide that?"

"When he asked her for her recipe."

"Let's not get hysterical just yet, if that's your only reason," Julie said. "He's probably just a potato-salad freak."

"I can't eat," Edie said. "You get some lunch. I'll go pick his green peppers."

"Throw in some onions, too," Julie said. "It couldn't hurt."

Edie ran to the garden and picked three of the brightest, greenest peppers she could find. Then she dug up four onions and dropped them in the bag, too.

"These'll be perfect," Jake said when she came back in and gave them to him. "Someday I'll have to make some—" The crack of a bat against a ball made Jake lean sideways in his chair to see around Edie. She stepped quickly out of his way and started collecting dirty paper plates.

"You know how it is with men and baseball," Julie said, following Edie to the kitchen sink. "You might as well give in gracefully."

"I'll be darned if I'm going to watch it all afternoon, though. He probably won't even talk to Kate while the game's on." Edie threw the plates into the garbage can. "We could go up and play Scrabble. Maybe he'll miss me when I'm gone."

"I don't know. You'll just cream me again. Remember the last time we played? You got a seven-letter word. But I've forgotten what it was."

"Eclipse. One of my better moves on a triple."

"Oh, yeah, that's right. And now it looks like you've been eclipsed by a lousy ball game," Julie said. "The end of another of Edie Edmunds's famous romances."

"Oh, just shut up," Edie said.

Edie won the first game of Scrabble, and they were well into a rematch and halfway through a pitcher of lemonade when the truck started up in the driveway. Edie flew to her window. Michael was behind the wheel, and Jake was standing by the truck, waving good-bye to someone out of sight on the porch below. "Tell Edie thanks again for me, will you? Lunch was great."

"Kate's lunch was great," Edie said, mimicking Jake's enthusiasm. "I knew I should've gone back downstairs. I thought baseball games lasted longer than this." She sat back down on her bed, studying the word Julie had just played. "I'll bet Jake will call me later tonight, right after he chops up the vegetables," she said. "Or maybe he'll wait and call me tomorrow. That'd be OK, too. You wait and see. Jake just didn't want to get too passionate with my whole family watching, that's all. He only talked to Kate because he likes potato salad."

"I knew you'd come around," Julie said. She picked up her glass of lemonade and held it up to Edie's. "To the famous storm," she said. "When first these two met."

Edie clinked her glass against Julie's, and the girls bent toward each other, laughing hard.

Chapter Seven

"Excuse me," Edie said as she left her customer to answer the store phone. It was Julie.

"I'm with someone," Edie said. "I can only talk a second."

"OK," said Julie, "I'll talk fast. I'm at the beach, baby-sitting for J.J. III and his friend Robby. Robby's mother is taking over around twelve-thirty. Could you get away for lunch?"

"We're pretty busy today," Edie said. "And I brought a lunch from home."

"C'mon! My treat. We'll just get a slice of pizza. It'll only take two minutes to eat. Has Jake called yet?"

"No . . ." Edie hedged.

"I'm sorry," said Julie.

"Listen, pick me up when you're through, OK?" Edie said. "But we'll have to eat fast."

"It'll be about quarter to," Julie said.

Edie's customer was standing by the counter with a book in her hand. Edie hung up the phone and went to the cash register. "This one'll do," the woman said.

"May I gift wrap it for you?" asked Edie, after the woman had paid for the book.

"Oh, yes," said the woman. "That'd be great."

Edie took a package of paper out of a drawer. "Is this OK?"

"Wonderful. And would you have a little gift card?"

Edie opened another drawer and handed the woman a small gift-enclosure card that matched the paper. The woman beamed as Edie finished tying on yellow ribbon. "I love the service here," the woman said. "I will definitely come in again."

"Please do," Edie said, walking the woman to the front door.

"I'll tell everybody on the lake about this wonderful shop."

"Do warn them about the smut, though." Virginia Lamoreaux tapped the woman on the shoulder imperiously and sailed through the doorway. Crystal was at her heels. *Oh, no,* Edie thought, *they snuck up on me!*

When the customer left, Edie whirled around to see if Virginia had spotted Miss Harriet, who was trapped in her little office by the back door. Virginia was blocking the doorway, and Miss Harriet was behind her typewriter, a polite smile frozen on her face.

Edie sighed and walked over to Crystal. In between the shelves of children's books were displays of stationery, cards, and a few odd, expensive holiday decorations. Crystal was examining a tiny six-piece band of musicians on the Christmas table. Last week it had been a seven-piece band, but the tiny music rack had vanished, and Edie hadn't been able to find it anywhere. Crystal gave Edie a frail little smile and hurried past her down the aisle toward her sister. Edie glanced at the band. Only five! Now the tuba player was gone. *Funny,* Edie thought. *Was Crystal by this table last Thursday? With all the Lamoreaux money, was Crystal a shoplifter?*

Edie wandered closer to Miss Harriet's office. Miss Harriet squeezed past Virginia and turned to face her. "As I said, I'm sorry you disapprove, but you've got no business disapproving when you've never read a romance novel in your life."

"I think I see Harriet's point," Crystal whispered.

"I give up on both of you!" Virginia said. "Crystal, you, especially, should be ashamed! Harriet, I do hope you've at least managed to get that copy of *The Prophet* I ordered two weeks ago. Cameron's wedding is Saturday."

Edie shook her head as Miss Harriet looked at her questioningly. "It didn't come in yet," Edie said, "but there's still a copy on the shelf."

"I know there's a copy on the shelf," Virginia snapped. "And the dust jacket's torn and dirty!"

"I'm sorry," Miss Harriet said. "But I don't understand why you worry about dust jackets. You never leave the jacket on any book you're giving as a gift. It just isn't done."

"It isn't?" Virginia, speechless for once, trotted after Edie as she found the book, then watched her like a hawk to make sure she threw the dust jacket away. Edie had to look away from Miss Harriet to keep from giggling. Instead, she concentrated on folding neat corners and tying a fancy bow.

When the Lamoreaux sisters had been collected by their chauffeur, Edie and Miss Harriet both burst out laughing. "Fast thinking, huh?" Miss Harriet said, wiping tears of laughter out from under her glasses.

"You're one up on Virginia, Miss Harriet, but I think there's a problem with Crystal. She was fiddling with that band set, and now the tuba player's missing. I'll bet she took him home to go with the music rack."

"Oh, no," Miss Harriet said. "I don't know what I'd do if I caught her red-handed. Honestly, it must be an awful life, putting up with Virginia day in and day out."

"I'll watch her more closely next time," Edie said. "And I think I'll move the band."

"Mark it down a touch more, too. Whatever you think a tuba player's worth." Miss Harriet looked at her watch. "Where'd the morning go? You go to lunch. I can handle the people who're left here."

"Would you mind going first? I told Julie I'd eat with her a little later."

Miss Harriet dug her purse out from under the morning's mail. "Virginia has spoiled my appetite for grilled cheese, for some reason. I'll have to try something else today. Forty-five years of lunch at Jesperson's and I doubt I've ever seen a menu."

"Forty-five years? You mean you were only twenty when you opened Book Bayou?"

"Around about," Miss Harriet said. If she really was seventy, as Gus Hartwick had said, she wasn't about to admit it. "Wave a red flag if you need me back. I'll get a window table." Miss Harriet punched open the cash register and took out a ten-dollar bill.

"Oh, don't worry. I can take care of things."

"First summer help I haven't worried over in ages," Miss Harriet said, "if the truth be told. Remind me to get to the bank and cash a check. I keep running out of money."

"Go to the bank and cash a check," Edie said.

"Later, kiddo. I meant remind me later." Miss Harriet waved to the UPS man just coming in and scooted out of the store.

Edie was taking her first mouth-scorching bite of pizza when the door of the pizza place wheezed closed.

"Don't look now," Julie whispered, from the other side of the booth, "but it's the original Wonder Boy himself."

Edie swallowed a mouthful without chewing it. "Is he with Liza?"

"No, he's alone," Julie said. "Now he's placing his order. Now he's walking our way. Nope. He's going to have a game of Asteroids first."

"Maybe he won't notice us. It's pretty crowded today."

The blips and beeps of the electronic game faded, and Edie heard a chair scrape away from a table behind her.

"Bingo!" Julie whispered. "He's just decided he recognizes the back of your head."

The chair scraped again, and Sean came over to their booth. His face was tanned, and his blond hair shone silver in the light from the Tiffany lamp overhead. He smiled at Edie. She could smell Sean's coconut tanning oil over the smell of oregano coming from the kitchen.

"Where's Liza?" Julie asked immediately.

"Liza?" Sean's look of studied innocence amazed Edie.

"Yeah, Liza Melsheimer," Julie said. "You have heard of her?"

"Oh, sure, Liza. She's away for a week. Her grandmother got sick. Something like that. You two want to hit the beach with me this afternoon?"

"I don't think Liza would like that," Julie said.

"Plenty of me to go around. Liza'll have to realize that."

"I have to work," Edie said.

"You mean that old battle-ax wouldn't spring you for one perfect afternoon like this? How about if I go back with you and ask her myself?"

Edie snatched up her shoulder bag and slid out of the booth, not bothering to finish her pizza. "I happen to love my job," she said, her voice trembling with anger, "and I really don't care what you think about Miss Harriet." She rushed out the door and through the traffic back to Book Bayou, with Julie right behind her.

"Are you all right?" Miss Harriet asked worriedly as the girls ran in.

Edie was shaking. "Oh, I ran into someone who makes me sick," she said.

"Ahhh, I see!" Miss Harriet said. "Well, get out of my way and wait just a minute. A nice cold Seven-Up will calm you down."

Miss Harriet went to the basement, retrieved a soda from the little refrigerator down there, and brought it to Edie.

"I can see why you love this job," Julie said, following Edie and Miss Harriet back to their customers.

Edie grinned at Julie as she sidestepped her way through the line at the cash register and flashed their special "catch-you-later" sign.

Between customers, Edie kept checking the

street outside to see if Sean's car was still there. When Sean finally did come out of the pizza place, he didn't even glance toward Book Bayou. Edie felt herself flush and tried to conjure up Jake's laughing brown eyes. *Jake's the one boy I know worth liking,* Edie told herself. *Sean shouldn't be able to upset me anymore. Not when I finally have realized what a turkey he is. Now if only Jake would call me . . .*

Chapter Eight

Early that evening, Edie was curled up on the sofa in the living room, deep in a book, when she heard her father call to someone. Edie looked out the window. It was Jake. A pie plate in one hand, he was leaning against the porch railing, talking to her father. *Something's different about Jake. He looks so different.*

His beard was gone! Jake's face looked weird; it was tan on top and bluish-white from his cheekbones down. "I hardly recognized you," Edie said, as she hurried to the front door. "Why'd you get rid of it? C'mon in."

Jake ran a hand over his chin. "Oh, I just wanted to see if I could grow one in the first place. I was starting to feel grubby behind it."

"Well, I liked it," Edie said. "How was your Chinese something-or-other last weekend?"

"It was a dish to remember," Jake said, "thanks to your peppers. I came over tonight to bring you something I made. I found some wild blackberries in the woods, and I whipped up a pie." Jake followed Edie and her father into the kitchen and put the pie down next to the sink where Mrs. Edmunds and Becky were cleaning snap peas. "I hope everybody likes blackberry pie," Jake said.

"Did you get the blackberries in our woods?" Becky asked. "The ones by the back road are ours."

"However, Beck," Mr. Edmunds said, "I don't notice you down there getting them picked."

Edie watched Jake's cheeks turn red. "I'm sorry," he said. "I just ran right into them while I was hiking around. I didn't pick all the ripe ones."

"Oh, don't pay any attention to Becky," Mrs. Edmunds said, glaring at her youngest daughter. "You can have all the berries you want."

Kate turned away from the oven, a turkey baster in her hand. "Since you brought dessert," she said, "why don't you stay and eat with us? Dinner's almost ready. Did you bring Doctor Paul along, too?"

"No, he got stuck at Game Haven today. But I'd love to stay. If you've got enough."

"A whole turkey," Kate said. "It's our Thanksgiving-in-July night."

Edie handed an extra plate and silverware to Jake, who set a place for himself at the corner of the table. "Is this all right?" he asked.

"Sure," Edie said. *Couldn't be better. You put yourself right next to me.*

"If you're not busy after dinner," Jake said, "maybe we could take Becky to the woods and let her pick the rest of the blackberries. I feel funny about picking your stuff."

"Don't be silly," Edie said. "They're only wild berries. But I'd like to go. It would be fun."

"You'll have to let me count my ladybugs first, though," Becky said, putting the bowl of hot peas by Jake's place. "I hope you'll eat snap peas, Jake," Becky said. "I made them all by myself."

"They look delicious," Jake said, grinning at Edie over Becky's head. "Will you let me have your recipe?"

"Sure." Becky giggled. "I'll write it on a card."

Jake's taking me to the woods! He didn't

ask Kate. He asked me! I knew that was just my imagination all along.

Jake talked mostly to Michael during dinner, but twice, passing her platters, his brown eyes brushed lightly over hers. He didn't talk to Kate at all, except to say he loved the cranberries she had put in the raspberry Jell-O. Which was not exactly a proposal, as Julie would say.

"I've got thirty-seven scratches and just one pail of berries," Becky said. "But I guess your pie was worth it."

"That pie was a masterpiece," Jake said. "And besides, you said we were even when I found that chrysalis for you. You said it was a fair trade for stealing your berries."

"You're such a pig sometimes, Becky," Edie said. "Come on and soak your scratches in the creek."

A sudden wind blew up as they walked back into the woods. The tops of the tall hardwoods swayed and rustled, and the pines began to whisper. "More rain's on the way," Jake said. "You can tell the trees have already seen it coming. Hear them discussing the weather?"

"I thought me and Edie were the only two people who could hear trees talk," Becky said. "I thought it was our secret."

"I guess now there are three of us," Jake said. He looked at Edie, and they smiled at each other.

"C'mon," Becky said. "Let's go see where I drownded."

"*Almost* drownded, you mean," Jake said. He pulled back the bough of a big blue spruce and waved Edie ahead of him through the gap. "Trees that talk, huh?" he said, as she brushed past. "I knew you were my kind of girl."

"It's crazy, I know," she said, "but on windy nights, I love to sit up late and just listen."

"I do my best thinking on nights like that," Jake said. "Let's sit up here while Becky splashes around." Jake dropped onto a grassy spot on the bank.

"I won't go near the waterfall," Becky hollered, "in case you were going to worry about it."

"I was," Edie said, "which is why we're right here where we can see you."

Jake leaned back on his elbows and raised his face to the sky. "Cloudy night. We won't have any stars."

"We shouldn't stay too long. Only long enough to let Becky clean up a little. She won't wear shoes, and she hates baths."

"She's a funny little kid," Jake said. "I like

her." He sat up and broke a switch off a dead aspen hanging overhead. "It's your big sister I can't figure out. I mean Kate seems so content to be cooking and cleaning and waiting on everybody. Doesn't she ever want to do anything else? Uncle Paul worries about her. He thinks she ought to move out and be on her own."

So that's what we're doing out here in the woods. He just wanted to pump me about Kate!

"Well," Edie said slowly, "you better not let on you know anything if I tell you. It's just that Kate's a little gun-shy right now. See, there was this rich summer guy who dumped her. Kate gets good secretarial jobs downtown every year, but she quit last summer and this so that she wouldn't run into Steve. I guess she'll get her own place once she gets over Steve."

"Steve must be something else. Uncle Paul was wondering why Kate didn't keep a job all year long."

"She will one of these days."

Jake was quiet, peeling bark off the switch. "Breaking up's not easy. Getting dumped is even worse." He whipped angrily at the grass with his stick.

"Did a rich girl dump you once? Because you don't have enough money?"

"Oh, I guess it was more of a mutual dump,"

Jake said. "And it wasn't because I do
money. It was more because I don't s]
like water the way Claire would've likeu. She
was always after me to buy new clothes and
everything." Jake plucked at his Levis. "You
can see I don't care much about how I look. But
Claire—you'd never catch her in plain old Levis.
Or eating at McDonald's. Every time we went
out to eat, it had to be the fanciest restaurant
in town."

"She sounds spoiled," Edie said. "How old
is she?" *Sixteen, let him say sixteen. No older
than that, oh, please!*

"Eighteen, going on twelve. She had her
last temper tantrum because I refused to go to
college in the East with her in the fall. Once I
decided on Michigan State, it was all over."

"That's a terrific school for veterinarians,"
Edie said. "Do you want to be a vet?"

"If I can get in, sure," Jake said. "It's worse
than dental school these days." He broke his
stick into bits and tossed them out into the
water. "So now you know the story of my life.
Uncle Paul's needing some help worked out perfectly for me. It's good experience, and I needed
to get out of town."

"I'm glad you decided to come," Edie said.

87

"I mean, Doctor Paul's needed somebody around for ages."

Jake cocked one eyebrow and grinned crookedly at Edie. "Sometimes I think I'm in a time warp or something. At least, it seems that way with the women I run into. I mean, first Claire turns out to be such a baby, and then you come along, sixteen going on twenty-five. It's weird."

Twenty-five! And I was worried you thought I was too young. Edie jumped to her feet, brushing off the seat of her jeans. "Becky! C'mon out! It'll be dark soon."

Jake stood up behind her and took hold of her elbows, turning her around. "Hey, I didn't mean I thought *you* were weird! Are you mad? I think sixteen going on twenty-five's great!"

"Of course I'm not mad! I—I just thought I'd better rush home and check for gray hairs."

Jake picked up a thick bunch of her golden hair and peered at it. "Too dark to say for sure, but I don't think you need to worry yet. Are we still friends?"

"Oh, of course! I'm not a baby, like Claire." She tossed her head so Jake had to let go of her hair.

"Hey," Jake said, "how about a movie this weekend?" He squatted down and pulled Becky up the bank. "We could even take Becky, here."

"Yes, you could," Becky said. "Edie keeps saying she'll take me, only she never has enough money saved up."

"See how terrific I am?" Edie said. "A regular Scrooge."

"You're perfect," Jake said. "Saturday night OK?"

"I'd love it!" Edie said. "I'll even spring for the popcorn."

"Should we ask Kate, too? It'd be good for her to get out of the house."

Kate again. "I'll ask her. But she probably won't come." Edie tried to smile, but the minute Jake looked at her, she knew he could see through it. Jake's puzzled eyes started to twinkle. "You're jealous, right? After I said sixteen going on twenty-five's perfect for me? How many times does a guy have to tell you something?"

Edie laughed. "Sorry, sorry!"

"I thought you two made me get out of the water because we were going home," Becky said.

Jake took Becky by one hand, Edie took the other, and they ran out of the woods and across the long pasture.

At the house Becky ran inside to put her chrysalis safely in a pickle jar. The sweet headiness of the mock orange bush under the kitchen window scented the cloudy night. Panting, Jake flopped on the bottom porch step. "You are one fast runner. I was going all out just to keep up."

"I'm really not so fast. It's just that I have long—"

At the same instant, Jake said, "It's just that you have long legs, I know, I know."

Our minds reached out and touched, Edie thought. *Touched and came up with the exact same words. Even Julie will have to admit that must mean something.*

Edie walked Jake to the jeep. "I better go make sure Uncle Paul's found himself something to eat, if he's gotten back yet," Jake said. "Thank your mom and dad again for feeding me."

"And thanks again for your pie," Edie said.

Jake's gentle smile seemed as bright as stars as he briefly stroked Edie's hair, tucking it behind her ears. Then he climbed into the jeep and drove away. Edie grinned up at the cloudy night sky. *Who needs moonlight? I think he likes me. I really think he does.*

Chapter Nine

Edie's hair whipped across her face as Jake sped down the road by the lake. Becky sat between them, her ponytails flying in the wind. At the Mitchell Street stoplight, Jake turned sideways and laughed at Edie. "You look as blind as a sheepdog. I should've warned you to bring a scarf. Jeep riding does wonders for long hair."

"You're lucky you have curly hair," Becky said. "Yours just sort of bounces around on your head."

"Oh, no! You saw me the night of the rain. It was so frizzed up I had to go through doorways sideways."

Edie laughed and brushed her hair back as Jake headed down the street toward the movie theater. *I could've remembered my yellow scarf on my own. To match my dress. Hard to believe now that I bought it just for Seán.*

"We're early," Jake said, leading the way to the ticket booth where he bought three tickets from old Mrs. Sykes, the cashier. "We'll have plenty of time to pick out some goodies."

Edie herded Becky ahead of her into the line for popcorn. "Treats are on me, remember?" Edie said.

"No way," said Jake. "This is my party. Who else have I got to spend my hard-earned wages on?"

"You have to save some for college this fall, don't you?"

Jake put his hands on Becky's shoulders to move her ahead in the line. "Dad had a college fund set up for me before I was an hour old," he said.

"Oh!" Edie said. "How neat!" *Jake did have money then. Funny he doesn't act rich, like Seán.* "But you'll have to let me buy seconds," Edie said. "Becky eats a lot at movies."

"Look who's talking!" Becky said. "You're the one who buys the giant popcorn so we can get the free refill. I want Junior Mints, and can I have the jumbo Coke, too?"

"If you get the jumbo, you'll be running to the bathroom all night," Edie said.

"Three jumbo Cokes, one giant popcorn, three Junior Mints," Jake said to the girl behind the counter. "That ought to hold us for a while."

Becky grinned triumphantly at Edie. "I'll sit in the middle and hold the popcorn," she said.

"I'll hold the popcorn," Edie said quickly. "You always spill it."

Jake found three seats midway down the center section of the theater. "Let Becky have the aisle, in case she has to go to the bathroom," he whispered to Edie. He settled into his seat, propping his knees on the seat in front of him. "It's too bad Kate wouldn't come along. She shouldn't hide out every summer. There must be something we can do to get her out of the house."

Edie sighed. "She was absolutely convinced Steve and his girl would be downtown tonight, and I couldn't change her mind. I bet she'd go to the beach up at Good Hart, though. It's usually fairly deserted."

"Well, let's try it." Jake sat up straight in his seat. "The movie's about to start. Do you have to go to the bathroom, Becky?"

"Well, not yet, for heaven's sake!" Becky said.

The lights dimmed, and the maroon curtain rose slowly.

Just before the theater was completely darkened, Edie saw Sean over in the left aisle edging past people to get to two seats at the end of the row. Liza squeezed by behind him, her white sleeveless jumpsuit shining faintly in the dimness. As Sean turned to unfold his seat, he looked up and saw Edie. Edie quickly turned to smile at Jake and took a fast sip of her Coke.

Halfway through the movie, Becky was on her third trip to the bathroom and hadn't returned to her seat. Edie moved the popcorn to Jake's lap. "I'd better see what's keeping Becky. I'll be right back."

Becky was in the lounge, watching in fascination as a woman glued on a pair of very long, very fake eyelashes. "These darn things are more trouble than they're worth," she said as Edie came in.

"C'mon, Beck!" Edie hissed. "We're missing everything." She ushered Becky out.

As Edie closed the lounge door behind her, she saw Sean just turning away from the snack stand. Two Eskimo Pies were balanced on top of a tub of popcorn.

"I thought I saw you," Sean said. "Having a family outing tonight?"

"Family outing?"

"Well, there's three of you," Sean said. "Is that Michael you're with? I don't know your brother very well."

Becky started to giggle. "Michael doesn't have orange hair! That's Jake! He's our date!"

"How about that?" Sean's eyes were amused as he turned to Edie. "What's the kid along for, then? You need a chaperon?"

"I'm part of the date!" Becky shouted.

"She's right, Sean," Edie said. "And, by the way, your ice cream's melting all over your popcorn."

"Shoot!" Sean grabbed for napkins, and Edie pushed Becky into the dark aisle, grinning to herself.

When the movie ended, Sean and Liza hurried to the exit at the back of the theater. Edie followed Jake out the front way. *Oh, well,* Edie thought, *one glimpse is all Sean's going to get of Jake. At least, for tonight. I hope he's good and jealous.*

"I want to sit by the door going home," Becky said. "I get more wind that way. I like how it takes your breath away."

"Be my guest," Jake said. His arm brushed Edie's as he shifted the jeep into drive. Jake's arm was warm, and the fine hairs on Edie's arm tingled. Jake drove slowly out of town, relaxing as he hit the lake road. "Look at that moon on the water. Pretty, isn't it?"

Edie brushed her flying hair out of her eyes so she could see. "Seventeen million stars, too. I love summer nights that look like they're supposed to."

Jake laughed and lifted his right arm over Edie's head, letting it fall across her shoulders. "I'm glad I headed north this summer," he said.

"Edie? Are you cold?" Becky asked.

"No. Why? Are you?"

"I'm boiling," Becky said. "I just wondered why Jake has his arm wrapped around you."

Jake tugged on Becky's ponytail. "I thought Edie might still be scared from the movie. Didn't you think it was scary?"

"You should go to the bathroom for the scary parts," Becky said. "That's what I do."

Jake checked his rear-view mirror, and Edie

saw his face turn grim. "There's a turkey coming up behind us like a bat out of you-know-where. Make sure Becky's seat belt is fastened."

Edie yanked on Becky's seat belt as Sean's little car swung around the jeep with a blast from its horn.

"Idiot," Jake said. Sean's taillights flashed brighter as he braked to turn off into the woods a hundred yards ahead. "Some summer guy who doesn't know how to drive off the interstate, I guess."

"No," Becky said, "those were just those movie-star friends of Edie's again."

"Really?" Jake said. "Friends of yours?"

"Not really," Edie said. "Just Sean and Liza, classmates from school. They're probably going to a party out at Weber Lake tonight."

"I didn't know that old road ended up anywhere," Jake said. "Is Weber Lake a good place for a picnic? I pack a mean picnic."

"It's a huge beaver pond really," Edie said. "I haven't been out there in a long time. I suppose it'd be a good place."

"Want to investigate it tomorrow? I'll bring all the food. Unless you're already busy."

"No, no, I'm not busy," Edie said. "It's a great idea."

"I love picnics," Becky said.

"The picnic's just for me and Edie, OK?" Jake said. "Besides, I want to check it out first. There might be big hairy spiders. Maybe even snakes."

"I love snakes and spiders," Becky said. "I love all animals and bugs. But I get it. You guys want to do all that lovey-dovey stuff."

"Becky!" Edie warned. "That's enough."

Jake chuckled and patted Edie's knee. "What'll I make? Barbecued chicken or plain fried?"

"Oh, barbecued, if you want to go to so much trouble. But let me bring something. The raspberries are still nice. I can make shortcake."

Jake turned into the driveway and stopped by the porch. "Sounds great. Don't spoil it by eating breakfast. I'll pick you up about twelve-thirty. Be ready for a feast."

Jake climbed out of the jeep, and Edie slid under the steering wheel, scrambling out behind him. "It's still early. Do you want to come in?"

"I'd like to, but I better get home. We'll have the whole afternoon together tomorrow, though, OK?"

"OK. Listen, thanks for the movie. It was great. I really enjoyed it."

"Me, too," Jake said. He swatted at a moth hovering around the porchlight. "I hate it when those things land in my hair."

"I'll bet they could stay trapped in there forever," Becky said. "Aren't you going to kiss us good night?"

"Becky! Jake, I'm sor—"

"Becky's absolutely right," Jake said. "As usual." He stooped and brushed Becky's cheek with a kiss. Then he took Edie by the shoulders and solemnly kissed her on the end of her nose. "There! Did I forget anything else?"

"Nope," Becky said. "Now you can go home."

"See you tomorrow," Jake said. His brown eyes shone with laughter in the moonlight. Edie laughed back at him and pushed Becky into the house. Tomorrow there would be real kisses. Maybe.

Edie crouched on the floor of the hall closet upstairs, winter coats tickling her nose, the telephone in her lap. "Jake is so fantastic, he really is," she said.

"You mean you've got the zing?" Julie said.

"Definitely. Guess who else was at the movies tonight? Besides us."

"You have to be kidding. With Liza?"

99

"Yep. Sean was getting food as I came out of the lounge, and he thought I was on a family outing with Michael and Becky."

"The turkey! Did you straighten him out?"

"Becky did. She said Jake was our date. And at the front door, she asked if Jake was going to kiss us good night!"

"So? Was he?"

"Well, finally, but only on my nose. It would've been different if Becky hadn't been there, I bet. Anyway, he's taking me on a picnic tomorrow, and he told Becky she couldn't come. Isn't that a good sign?"

"Look, just don't accept when he proposes, will you? You'll be a real drag next year if you're engaged."

"Come on, Julie, be serious for once."

"Well, really—I hope you have a great time tomorrow. Save me some leftovers, will you?"

"Barbecued chicken all right with you?"

"Ooh, that sounds so good! The next time Jake plans a picnic, get Dave and me invited, too."

"Oh, I think two's company on a picnic, don't you?"

"Boy! You really are in bad shape."

"At least, I *think* two's company. I'll let you know tomorrow night for sure."

Edie hung up the phone and smiled. She peeked out of the closet. Nobody was around. So she did three cartwheels down the hall, winding up in the center of her bedroom doorway.

Chapter Ten

The next morning Edie finished ironing her "Don't let the turkeys get you down" T-shirt. It was her favorite shirt. On it, little brown turkeys climbed all over a gray elephant, which was lying down. She pulled it over her head and tucked it into her jeans. She brushed out her hair again, then went downstairs and set the cooler—already filled with fresh raspberries, whipped cream, and soft, round shortcakes—by the back door. Then she turned to her gift-wrapping project set out on the kitchen table.

Miss Harriet had gone crazy over Edie's turkey T-shirt the last time she had worn it to work. So on Friday, Edie had slipped into the

T-shirt store on her lunch break and bought a beige one for Miss Harriet. Edie just knew Miss Harriet would wear it every Thursday, the day Virginia Lamoreaux came into town.

Mrs. Edmunds stopped slicing cucumbers to help Edie fold the shirt to fit into the gift box. "You must really like Miss Harriet to part with some of your hard-earned cash," she said. "But do you think it's appropriate? I mean, older women don't usually wear T-shirts."

"You don't know Miss Harriet, Mom. As long as it's some shade of green or brown, she'll wear it."

"We should invite her over for dinner one day. She's been so kind, letting you and Becky borrow all those books."

"I don't think she cares much about food. She only eats grilled cheese sandwiches."

"Maybe she doesn't bother to cook, living alone. What time is Jake picking you up?"

Edie tied a green ribbon on the package. "Any minute now. We're going out to Weber Lake."

"I guess that's all right as long as it's daylight. Don't let me hear about you out there after dark."

Edie felt her face get hot. "Oh, Mom, don't worry. Jake's very sensible. You know that."

"And so are you," Mrs. Edmunds said. "Dad and I were just saying last night what a lovely young woman you're turning into."

"Oh, Mother, please! I hear the jeep." Edie ran to the window just as the jeep bounced to a stop by the back steps.

Mrs. Edmunds opened the back door to let Jake into the kitchen. "Did anyone remember to pack the bug spray?" she asked.

"I did, if Edie didn't," Jake said. "I even packed a first-aid kit."

"I've got bug spray, too," said Edie. "The ants won't stand a chance today."

"Hey, great shirt," Jake said, reading Edie's chest.

Mentally Edie subtracted another six dollars from her savings. Should she buy him a large or an extra-large?

"This the dessert?" Jake asked, pointing to the cooler by the door.

"Yup," Edie said. "Let's go. I'm starved. I missed our special Sunday breakfast for this picnic."

"Well, you won't be hungry for long. Uncle Paul swiped half a chicken for himself, but that still leaves us a whole chicken and a half. And wait'll you see the rest of the stuff."

"See you later, Mom," Edie said. She brushed

past Jake and got a whiff of his spicy after-shave.

They walked outside and caught Becky emerging from under the snowball bush, shoe-box in her hand. She ran to the driveway and smirked at Jake. "Have fun," she said. "Say hello to the spiders and snakes for me."

"Sure thing, Beck," Jake said. "We might even save you a bite to eat."

Edie looked at the giant picnic basket and the big cooler in the backseat. "I guess! There's enough for an army. Go on back to your lady-bugs, Becky. And quit smirking!"

"What a character," Jake said, as he pulled out of the driveway. "I probably brought too much food, but I like to be prepared. Although I was a rotten Boy Scout."

"I was a rotten Brownie."

Jake turned onto the highway and started to whistle. The old logging road to Weber Lake was enclosed on both sides by tall red-raspberry bushes. The thorny branches scraped the sides of the jeep, and Edie moved closer to Jake. "We used to have a black Lab who leaned out the car window and grabbed for raspberries every time we came out here. She loved raspberries so much she never minded the thorns."

Jake laughed. "Hey," he said. "I can see

somebody's roof up that rise over there. I guess that'd be Mr. Hartwick's."

Edie nodded. "Could we stop in on the way back? I thought I had him talked into coming to town to buy books, but he's never shown up."

"Do you guarantee he won't chase us off with a shotgun?"

"I guarantee. He's my friend now."

"How much farther to this lake?"

"Just a few miles, I think." The jeep bounded along over the ruts, and they rode in silence, enclosed in a green, sweet-smelling tunnel, dappled with flecks of gold.

A wide, bare spot had been carved into an unofficial parking lot at the lake's shore. "This place really does get traffic," Jake said. "Let's make sure there's a good spot before we lug the stuff out."

"Oh, wow," said Edie, when they stepped out. "I can't believe it. Most of the beach has disappeared. You can't see the sand for the junk." The beach was covered with crushed soda cans and flattened potato-chip bags. Crumbling logs from beach fires littered the entire shoreline. "Let's go eat in our own woods. This place is depressing."

"Can we walk down to the beaver dam first? If you won't die of hunger?"

"Sure, but the beavers will have gone to ground after hearing the jeep. You won't see any."

"I just want to look." Jake led the way to the far end of the long, narrow lake, taking Edie's hand once to help her over a fallen tree. She was disappointed when Jake let go of her hand after they were safely across. The dam stretched across the width of the lake and was a six-foot-high jumble of branches in the center. "You can see where they've been working," Jake said, looking around.

Six slender aspens had been felled, their stumps chiseled to neat, fine points. "Let's give them a hand," Edie said. "We can toss these in the water for them, like room service."

Edie shoved a tree off toward the dam, and Jake dragged another one to the waterline. "They'll think good fairies have been here," Jake said.

When all six aspens were in the water, Jake dusted off his hands and grinned at Edie. "You're not such a rotten Brownie, after all. I can just see Claire entertaining herself like this."

Edie tried not to wince at the mention of

Claire's name. "Maybe she doesn't like beavers. Now can we go eat?"

A few minutes later, Jake had parked the jeep in the blackberry clearing. They carried the basket and the coolers to the creek. Jake snapped open a checkered tablecloth and spread it by the bank. Then he took two bright blue throw pillows out of the basket and tossed one to Edie. "In case of a nap attack after lunch," he said.

Then will he finally kiss me right? Edie looked at Jake's happy, open face. Then she knelt on the tablecloth and helped unload the basket.

Edie couldn't believe how much food Jake had fixed. And everything was so good! The deviled eggs had cashew nuts in them, and Edie ate four, along with almost half a chicken, plus olives, green and black, potato salad with radish roses on top, and sweet-and-sour three-bean salad, not to mention drinking her share of soda.

Jake beamed at her as she rolled over onto her back, clutching a pillow to her stomach. "I like a girl who can really eat," Jake said. "Claire worried over every bite she put in her mouth."

"Did she know about these picnics of yours? I won't eat for a week."

"Claire? Go on a picnic? No way." Jake threw the paper plates and napkins into a plastic garbage bag he took out of the basket. Edie stacked the remainder of the salads in the cooler. "Well, time for your shortcake," Jake said.

"You're kidding? Aren't you? Can't we rest a little first?"

"On picnics, you have to eat everything all at once. It's a rule," Jake declared. "Otherwise, the sun will put us to sleep, and when we wake up, it'll be time to go home, and we'll miss dessert completely."

"Right." Edie grinned. She fixed two paper plates of shortcake, heaping them with raspberries and whipped cream. She handed Jake a fork and took a bite of her dessert. "I can't believe I'm eating this."

"Must be all the fresh air," Jake said.

After they had finished eating the shortcake, Jake said, "Now I'm ready to rest."

Edie put the empty plates and soda cans into the garbage bag. "I want to go rinse off my face first. I must have barbecue sauce and raspberry juice from ear to ear."

"Me, too." Jake took two yellow washcloths out of the bottom of the basket. "Here we go. The bathroom's just down the bank."

"Washcloths, no less! I refuse to believe you were a lousy Boy Scout."

In a few minutes they were back at the tablecloth, their faces still wet with icy creek water. Jake punched up his pillow and stretched out on his back, face to the sun. He was quiet for a few seconds, then he said, "You sure do have noisy crickets around here. C'mon. Relax with me."

Cautiously Edie lay down beside him, folding her hands neatly across her stomach. "The frogs sound nicer," she said. "But of course they only sing at night."

"I am *so* full," Jake said.

"That was a terrific picnic." Edie had to close her eyes against the sun's brightness, but she wasn't at all drowsy. She lay stiffly, making sure her left leg and arm didn't touch Jake, yet wishing he would lean over and kiss her. She lay listening to the water. Somewhere a whippoorwill was singing. Edie turned her head slowly toward Jake and opened her eyes a little.

His chest was moving slowly up and down, and he seemed very relaxed. His mouth opened slightly, and he let out a gentle snore.

Edie laughed out loud. "Well! Sweet dreams to you, too, Jake," she whispered. Then she turned on her side, away from him, and watched a family of ants trying to lift a shortcake crumb over a wrinkle in the tablecloth. She didn't have the heart to spray them.

About an hour later, Jake awoke with a start. "Oh, boy! I'm great company. I really fell asleep, didn't I?"

"Oh, that's OK. I think I did, too." Edie yawned to make the lie good.

"Your mother'll think we fell in and drownded. Do you still want to stop at Mr. Hartwick's?"

"Sure. It'll just take a minute. Nobody worries that much about me, anyway."

"I wouldn't want your folks to think I was up to no good. If you know what I mean." Jake grinned slyly at her and waggled his eyebrows up and down like an old-time comic.

"How could they? You have such an honest face." Edie helped Jake fold the tablecloth, liking the tingle when her fingers touched his, loving his smile. *But what could it hurt if you leaned over and kissed me? Even just once would be OK.*

Mr. Hartwick didn't answer the door. "But his car's here," Edie said. "He has to be around some place."

"Maybe he's hiding," Jake said. "You're not supposed to drop in on a hermit."

"But what if he's hurt himself? What if he's sick? I'm going to try the door."

"What if it's locked?" Jake said.

Edie tried the doorknob, and it turned. She opened the door a crack. "Mr. Hartwick? It's me, Edie. Can I come in?"

A strange, strangled sound came in response and made Jake shove the door open wide and charge inside. Mr. Hartwick was on the floor, his head under a table. He flapped one hand weakly at Edie as she hurried to kneel beside him. "Your fault," he muttered. "Was getting set to go buy a book." His speech was slurred, and one side of his mouth had a twisted look.

Jake leaned over Mr. Hartwick, loosening his tie. "How long have you been lying here? Get an ambulance, Edie."

Edie rushed to the phone and dialed the hospital.

"What's today?" Mr Hartwick said, as Edie knelt beside him again. "Saturday is it? Got dizzy a while back."

"It's already Sunday!" Edie said. "The ambulance is on the way. Oh, I'm sorry I tried to get you into town! You got all dressed up and everything."

"Too darn much fuss," Mr. Hartwick said,

fumbling at the edges of the blanket Jake was drawing up to his shoulders.

"I've got a cold pack for that bump on your head," Jake said. "It's just outside in the jeep. We'll be right back." He pulled Edie to her feet and hurried her outside. "It looks to me like he's had a stroke. You better go stand out in the middle of the road and wave the ambulance in here so they don't miss the place."

Edie ran. Her feet felt numb and heavy, and every rut in the path seemed determined to trip her up. When she finally reached the old logging road, she stood on tiptoe, straining to hear the sound of a siren.

Oh, please, let him be all right. Please. She wrapped her arms around herself and shivered in the sun.

Chapter Eleven

Edie grabbed the broom off the ledge beside the basement steps and began sweeping furiously. "Anyway, Miss Harriet, he looked just terrible. He was so gray. Before the ambulance took him away, he squeezed my hand real hard. But his right hand wouldn't work at all, only his left. If only I hadn't pestered him about coming to town."

"Nonsense," Miss Harriet said. "Gus is an old man. And you said it wasn't a serious stroke. He'll be all right in a few days." Miss Harriet cracked open a new roll of dimes and spilled them into the register. "You say he was all gussied up?"

"The works—tie, white shirt, jacket, everything. I've never seen him wear anything but that old plaid jacket before."

"I'll bet he'll give those poor nurses a time. Knowing how much he hates any fuss."

"I want to buy him a book. Dad and I are going to stop and visit him after work. What shall I bring?"

"Take him that new Civil War thing," Miss Harriet said. "I'll sell it to you at cost. Gus always was crazy about the Civil War."

"Really?" Edie said. "How do you know that?"

"Seems to me it was the Civil War, anyway." Miss Harriet tucked a pile of catalogs under one arm and stuck a pencil behind her ear. "If it wasn't, he can bring it back. I've got to get busy. All these specials have to get out today."

"Oh, wait! I nearly forgot. I have a present for you." Edie leaned the broom against a shelf and took the present out from under her sweater lying on the counter.

"My birthday's in May," Miss Harriet said. "Besides, you shouldn't spend your money on me. I don't pay you enough."

"So it's a late birthday present," Edie said. "Open it."

Miss Harriet stripped off the gift-wrapping

116

and lifted the shirt out of the box. "My own turkey shirt! How about that? Beige, too. Just my color. Thanks, kiddo." Miss Harriet pecked Edie on the cheek.

"I'll wear mine this Thursday if you'll wear yours," Edie said.

"You've got a deal. Maybe Virginia will get the message." Miss Harriet held the shirt up thoughtfully. "Edie? You don't suppose anybody in town still carries a plain, old-fashioned nightshirt?"

"Oh, do you need nightgowns? Penney's is having a sale, and they might have some."

Miss Harriet flapped her hands and shook her head. "No, no, I haven't any time for that today. Just a thought. I'd better get cracking."

Edie watched Miss Harriet hurry toward her typewriter, and then she went back to the stairwell for the dustpan. *Miss Harriet in a nightshirt!*

Later, as she was gift wrapping Mr. Hartwick's Civil War book, she started thinking again about Miss Harriet and Gus. Nobody could just pull that Civil War stuff out of thin air. A person had to know another person pretty well to know something like that. Tonight, she'd watch Mr. Hartwick when he opened the book. If he really was a Civil War freak, it would show, wouldn't it?

An hour later, Edie was behind the counter, selling a man a guide to northern Michigan mushrooms, when Miss Harriet waved at her from the other room. She had a stack of envelopes in one hand and her purse in the other. "I've got to go mail these. And buy stamps. And maybe get some coffee. I might be gone awhile."

"Take your time," Edie called. When the customer had left, Edie opened the drawer under the cash register where Miss Harriet kept paper clips and rubber bands. There were already three rolls of first-class stamps tucked neatly into one corner. She had enough to get through Christmas.

It was nearly one o'clock when Miss Harriet rushed back into Book Bayou, looking flushed, a foolish smile on her face. "Sorry to be so long, kiddo. I decided to try a new place for lunch as long as I was out. The service was terrible."

"I wasn't very busy," Edie said. "Just enough people so I couldn't get the dusting done."

"Oh, don't bother with it. Listen, after you get your lunch, I want you to run over to the wholesale place and bring back a bunch of the latest paperbacks. Whatever looks good."

"Great. I love to go there." Edie tied her

sweater around her shoulders and grabbed her lunch bag. "I'll be out back in the park if you need me."

Edie sat on a bench near the old cannon, which was crawling with kids as usual. She watched them play while she ate and tried to talk herself out of buying Jake a turkey shirt. After all, he hadn't bought anything for her yet. Maybe it was too soon for presents. She didn't want to embarrass him. But by the time she finished her lunch, she had decided to buy the shirt after all.

The T-shirt store was crowded, and Edie had to get in line to have the transfer ironed on. Maybe she could say it was her way of thanking him for the movies and the picnic. And she wouldn't have to give it to him immediately. The right moment was bound to come along. Edie's turn finally came, and ten minutes later she was walking back to Book Bayou, gift box in hand.

On her way to the wholesale place, Edie ducked into the combination drugstore/newsstand to check out the stock of paperbacks, wanting to be certain Book Bayou wasn't missing anything. The first person she saw was Liza Melsheimer, squirting herself with the sample perfumes while the clerk behind the cosmetics counter wrapped her purchase. Liza was wearing a tennis dress edged in pink lace. The fluffy balls on the back of her tennis socks matched the lace. Edie turned her back and tried to memorize the titles of the paperbacks on display.

Watching the door out of the corner of her eye to see if Liza was leaving, Edie suddenly smelled a combination of Charlie, Shalimar, and Je Reviens behind her. "Hey, Edie," Liza said. "I'm glad I ran into you."

"Hi, Liza," Edie said warily.

"Say, who was that guy you were with Saturday night? Sean said his name was Jake. I've never seen him around before."

"He's a college guy, from downstate," Edie said. "He's Doctor Duncan's nephew, and he's up here working for him this summer."

"Oh. That orange hair is very—interesting," Liza said off-handedly. "Does he have a perm?"

"No! It's naturally curly. And it's not orange! It's rusty brown."

"Oh," said Liza again, flatly. "Well, whatever. You and Jake enjoy yourselves. I'm already late for tennis with Sean." Liza bounced out of the store, leaving Edie fuming with rage.

*   *   *

Edie had good luck at the wholesale store. She bought a whole carton of books, including a couple of romances she intended to put out just to bug Virginia.

A cool breeze was blowing as Edie stepped outside, and she set the carton down long enough to put her sweater on. As she started across the street, she saw a bright, rusty-brown head of curls bobbing along ahead of her. Edie hurried after Jake, poking him in the back with her carton as she caught up to him. She started to laugh as Jake turned around.

"That box must be heavy," Jake said. "Let me be of assistance."

Edie pulled the carton away from him. "I'm the kid who tosses aspen trees into beaver ponds, remember? How come you're not working?"

"Uncle Paul didn't have any surgery scheduled, so he sent me on errands. One thing I have to do is order a birthday cake for him, only that's a surprise. I'm going to make him a Mexican dinner Saturday night. I want your family to join us."

"I'll ask," Edie said. "I'm sure everybody'd love to. I'll bring Doctor Paul one of these." She took out a book of cat cartoons and handed it to Jake.

Jake leafed through it as they waited at the intersection for the light to change. "He'll love it. This guy'll remind him of Oscar."

"Come on in with me and see Book Bayou. It's only a few more doors down, and then the bakery's just up around the corner. You can meet Miss Harriet."

"OK, but you'll have to let me carry that carton. What'll she think if you come in lugging that and I'm right behind carrying nothing?"

Edie shoved the carton at him. "I thought you liked strong, sensible, liberated women."

Jake grinned. "You better believe it," he said. "Especially when they've also got a little spark of romance in their souls."

"Well, maybe a little," Edie said. The zing was definitely getting stronger.

"By the way, I called to check on Mr. Hartwick this morning. The stroke didn't do any permanent damage at all."

"I'm just glad we found him when we did," Edie said. "Dad and I are going to visit him tonight." They reached the store. "Well, here's where I hang out. Is it OK if I open the door for you? Nobody's looking."

Jake shrugged. "I guess, considering I've got this huge box and everything."

Miss Harriet was perched on the edge of

one of the easy chairs, opening the mail and talking to a customer who was looking at Christmas card catalogs. She came over to the counter as Jake put the carton down on a bare spot Edie had cleared. "Thank you, kind sir," Miss Harriet said. "I knew there were gentlemen left somewhere in the world!"

Jake grinned at Edie, an I-told-you-so glint in his eye. "I wanted to meet you. Edie talks about you all the time."

"Does she now?" Miss Harriet beamed at Jake.

"This is Jake Duncan. Doctor Paul's nephew," Edie said.

Miss Harriet shook his hand. "You'd be Ben's son then? The Grosse Pointe branch of the family, if my memory serves."

Jake nodded. "Did you know my dad?"

"I knew your grandpa best. But Ben did wash windows for me one summer. Hard to believe he's got a grown-up son."

"I'll tell him I saw you," Jake said. "I hate to dash off, but I've got a lot of errands to run."

"I'll call you about Saturday night," Edie said as she began unloading the new books.

"Thanks again for the helping hand," Miss Harriet said. "Come in again. Anytime."

Miss Harriet waited until they saw Jake

striding past the windows outside before she spoke again. "Surely he's not the stomach-turner from the pizza place, is he? He seems a pleasant sort."

"No, the stomach-turner was somebody else. Jake is—fantastic!"

Miss Harriet leaned over to whisper in Edie's ear. "You could do much worse, you know. Jake's filthy rich."

"You're kidding. Filthy rich?"

Miss Harriet raised her eyebrows. "I'm not kidding. But if Jake is anything like his father, not much gets spent."

The customer looking at the catalogs cleared her throat in irritation, and Miss Harriet hurried over to take her order.

Edie finished arranging the new paperback display and tossed the carton down the basement stairs to carry to the garbage bin later. Then she got her feather duster and went into the other room to dust the picture books, wondering why it was that some rich people were so obnoxious and other rich people were so nice.

Edie's sandals clicked along the linoleum of the hospital corridor as she walked beside her father toward Mr. Hartwick's room. Mr. Edmunds had a small box of chocolates with him.

"I'll bet he's not allowed to have candy, Dad," Edie said.

"He can bribe the nurses with it," her father answered, smiling.

Mr. Hartwick's room had two beds in it, but the one near the door was empty. Edie walked around the separating curtain and found Mr. Hartwick propped up against pillows in his bed. The TV was on, and he was watching the news. When he saw Edie, he reached for the remote control device with his left hand and switched the set off. "Other hand's no darn good yet," he said, pushing himself upright with his left arm.

Edie gasped as he straightened up. He was wearing a white cotton nightshirt with a gray elephant and brown turkeys on the front. " 'Don't let the turkeys get you down'!" Edie said. "I love it, Mr. Hartwick. And I'll bet I can guess who got it for you."

"A friend," Mr. Hartwick said. "An old one." His eyes warned Edie to hold her tongue, but there was a twinkle in them.

Mr. Edmunds put the box of chocolates down on Mr. Hartwick's dinner tray, which still held a full dish of green and orange Jell-O cubes and a bowl of white glop that smelled like Cream of Wheat. "I know what the food's like around here. Maybe these'll taste a little better. They're from all of us, but especially Becky."

Mr. Hartwick eyed the chocolates. "Thank you," he said. "The food is pretty rotten, but I won't starve for a couple days, I guess. Which is all the more they're going to keep me."

"Really?" Edie said. "That's great."

"If I have my way about it," Mr. Hartwick said.

"I brought you something, too," said Edie, laying the book on the bed near his left hand. Mr. Hartwick fumbled with the ribbon and the paper and finally opened the package using just one hand. He looked at the title for a long time, and when he looked up, Edie could see his eyes watering. "Mighty nice thought," he muttered. "Mighty nice."

"I knew you'd like it! And I am sorry about trying to get you to come to town. I really am."

"Now don't worry," Mr. Hartwick said. "I'm just wearing out, that's all."

"Well, Gus, we just wanted to check in," Mr. Edmunds said. "I've got to get home to do the milking. Anything need checking at your place?"

"Not a thing. And please tell that young fellow with the orange hair thanks for me, if you should see him."

"I will, Mr. Hartwick," Edie said. "Jake was glad he could help." *But it's rusty brown,* she thought to herself. *Not orange.*

Edie glanced back at Mr. Hartwick from the doorway. A nurse had snapped back the curtain and was picking up his dinner tray. Mr. Hartwick grabbed the chocolates off the tray, glared at the nurse, then turned to the first page in his new book.

Chapter Twelve

Miss Harriet was already unpacking a shipment of cookbooks when Edie dashed into the store the next morning. "You didn't have to make it such a big secret about going to see Mr. Hartwick yesterday! I knew you'd been there the minute I saw his nightshirt."

"Don't be ridiculous," Miss Harriet said. "A woman my age doesn't give a man a nightshirt. It wouldn't be proper."

Edie took an armload of cookbooks and followed Miss Harriet into the other room. "Not for Virginia Lamoreaux it wouldn't, but maybe it is for you! Besides, who else would've thought of the turkeys?"

Miss Harriet placed each cookbook carefully on the shelf, making a neat row. "How you run on, kiddo. That could've come from anyone who knows how much Gus hates a lot of people fussing around him."

"He doesn't have any friends but us! And you, of course."

Miss Harriet tilted her head and looked at Edie through the bottom half of her bifocals. "I wouldn't take that strange old man a present if he were the last person on earth. How'd he like your book?"

"He cried when he opened it. It was funny how you managed to pick out just the perfect thing when you hardly know him. . . ."

"That's one of the reasons I've stayed in business so long," Miss Harriet said. "Sort of a sixth sense I've got. So the old coot really cried?"

"Well, his eyes got wet. And he was already starting to read it when I left. Come on, Miss Harriet, tell me! He used to—you and he were—come on, wasn't he once your—your boyfriend?"

"Boyfriend!" Miss Harriet's eyes snapped. "I'll leave boyfriends to you, kiddo," she said. "And how do you expect to have any money for college if you don't start earning your keep around here?" She took Edie by the shoulders and pointed her toward the basement doorway so she could get out her broom.

"OK, OK, have it your way. But I'd bet a million dollars Mr. Hartwick has been in love with you forever and you've always been crazy about him, too, only you probably had some stupid fight way back, and he married somebody else just to get even. He's been regretting it all these years, but he's just too proud to tell you so."

Miss Harriet stepped in front of Edie, her arms full of more cookbooks. "You know what, kiddo?" she said. "You read too many books." But she was smiling.

Julie appeared in the front door just as Edie was going out the back way with her lunch. "Hurry up," Edie called. "You can share my sandwich."

"I already ate," Julie said, waving to Miss Harriet as she crossed the store. "I have to baby-sit at two. I just wanted to hear some more about your picnic."

Edie settled herself on her favorite bench, and Julie sat down in the grass. "You already heard it all," Edie said. "Jake fell asleep, and then there was the mess with Mr. Hartwick, and that was it. But at least he wants to see me again. I ran into Jake downtown yesterday, and he invited our family to Doctor Paul's birthday party."

Julie took a bite of Edie's granola bar. "Sounds real romantic so far. I hope it's not for Friday night. Friday night I need you to sleep over at my house."

"The party's Saturday, so I can stay Friday." Edie took another bite of her cheese sandwich. "What's the big emergency?"

"Oh, Mom and Dad are spending the weekend at Birchwood. And I'm stuck with J.J. till Sunday afternoon. Dave's going to be over Saturday, but I don't want to be by myself Friday night."

"You're kidding! Dave's staying over Saturday night?"

"Of course not," Julie said. "He's only staying till midnight. He and J.J. have plans to watch a Three Stooges revival on TV. They'll have a ball, and by the time I go to bed, I'll be too tired to get nervous."

"Why in the world are your parents going to Birchwood? It's such an expensive resort."

"Well, Dad thinks he's going so he can try out their golf course, but Mom says she's going so she can talk to Dad for one whole weekend without J.J. butting in."

"They could lock their bedroom door and talk at home, for free." Edie crumpled up her lunch bag and tossed it into a trash can. "Want some of my apple juice?"

"No, thanks. Oh, you know how it goes at my house. Dad's usually out of town on business, and when he's home, J.J. won't let him out of his sight. Anyway, my mom's into communication these days. She's driving us all crazy."

"I'm beginning to think love without words is the only way to go," Edie said. "You ought to tell your mother that. The romantic part is how much you can tell about the other person's feelings without anybody saying anything definite at all. I think maybe talking about love all the time makes it too—too dry."

"What do you mean?" Julie asked curiously.

"I don't know. It's like books have to have words, but I don't know if people do. Look at Miss Harriet and Mr. Hartwick. She still won't admit they were even friends once, but I can tell she loves him! And the way Mr. Hartwick just about cried over that Civil War book. He knew Miss Harriet was behind that present. That's what brought the tears to his eyes . . . that she remembered what things mattered to him."

Julie was quiet for a long time. Finally

she smiled over at Edie. "I think you're really strange," she said softly. "That's what I think."

"Well," Edie said, "what if I am? I have to get back to work."

"I'll pick you up at the store Friday, and we can walk to my house together, OK? I hope that gourmet chef of yours hasn't spoiled your appetite for my macaroni and hot-dog super-supper."

"Don't be silly," Edie said. "By the way, if I can borrow a cookbook, would your mom care if we practiced a fancy dessert or something? I've just got to learn to cook. I'd die if I ever had to feed Jake anything."

"Why not? It'll be fun. See you Friday."

Edie turned back to Book Bayou, smiling as a fresh breeze blew in off the lake and lifted her bangs off her face. For an instant, she pictured Jake, asleep on a tablecloth in the woods, his eyelashes making spiky shadows on his cheeks. Then through the back window she saw that Book Bayou had filled up with customers. She flipped her hair under at her shoulders and hurried inside to help Miss Harriet.

At eight-thirty the next morning the sky was leaden, and fog rolled down the main street.

Edie waved goodbye to her father and crossed the street to Book Bayou.

Miss Harriet was blowing on charcoal in the fireplace. "It's going to be a busy Thursday," she said. "Looks like just enough rain's on the way for some good business." Miss Harriet fiddled impatiently with the kindling and some matches. "I can't get this dratted stuff to light."

Edie stuck a few more slivers of wood under the charcoal and added several crumpled pages of newspaper. Soon a little fire was dancing between the gray bricks.

"Doesn't warm us up all that much, but it looks pretty," Miss Harriet said. "I sure hope you plan to work here Saturdays after school starts. Otherwise, I won't be able to have a fire all winter long."

"I'll work as long as you want me to," Edie said.

"Even when you're in college, you'll need a summer job. By then, I'll just stay home with my feet up and let you run the whole show."

Edie smiled. "You'll never stay home with your feet up."

Miss Harriet sighed and rubbed the bridge of her nose under her glasses. "Rain makes my

135

bones ache," she said. "I'm not at all the woman I used to be."

Edie looked at her. "I think you look just fine. I'll go roll the awnings down before the rain starts. That'll give people a place to stay dry."

"You learned everything you know from me," Miss Harriet said. "Give them a place to stay dry, and they'll have to come in and buy." She shrugged off her sweater, revealing her turkey shirt underneath.

"Oh, good! I've got mine on, too." Edie peeled off her yellow sweater and tucked her shirt into her blue wraparound skirt. "You watch. This'll be the one Thursday Virginia Lamoreaux won't come to town."

"Well, stick out your chest, anyway," Miss Harriet said.

Edie took care of the awnings, then went to the basement to get several folding chairs to accommodate people picking Christmas cards. As she dragged the chairs out of their corner, she heard the first raindrops pinging on the old coal chute cover overhead. She dusted the cobwebs off the chairs and carried them upstairs. Within the hour, Book Bayou was crammed with people whose plans for the beach and the golf course and the sightseeing boat had been rained out. Miss Harriet stayed out on the floor, happily selling book after book, while Edie manned the cash register.

Around two, Edie dashed downstairs and sliced up an apple and a block of cheddar cheese for Miss Harriet's lunch. When she brought up the plate, the store had emptied of all customers but one. The woman looked at Edie as she carried Miss Harriet's lunch to the fireplace. "Oh, there you are, dear," the woman said. "I just dashed into town to buy my children some books to keep them out of my hair. All this rain!"

"Oh, hi," Edie said, recognizing the woman who had liked her gift wrapping earlier in the summer. "Do you want those gift wrapped?"

The woman considered. "Yes, I think so." She held up a mystery book for boys. "This is for my Bobby. Have you got any baseball paper?"

Edie managed to find some baseball paper, as well as three other patterns the woman liked. It took quite a while, but finally the woman left the store, each book done up in its special paper, each tied with a different color ribbon.

"Miss Harriet, you know everyone else in town charges for special gift wraps. Why don't you?"

Miss Harriet was staring into the fire, nibbling on a piece of cheese. *Probably remembering Mr. Hartwick,* Edie thought. *Wishing she hadn't let so many years slip by.* "Miss Harriet?"

"What was that, kiddo? Afraid I was out gathering wool."

"Nothing, really," Edie said. "I'll go downstairs and eat. Call me if you get busy."

Downstairs, Edie spread her lunch out on the worktable and read the front page of the previous Sunday's *New York Times* as she ate. She could see herself, a few years older, as a famous reporter rushing copy to her editor, and she could hear the man shrieking, "Stop the presses! I've got the next Pulitzer right here in my hands!" Edie read through the entire first section before she realized she had finished her lunch fifteen minutes before.

The store was filled with customers again. Miss Harriet, behind the cash register, was waiting on three people at once.

"Who's next?" Edie asked. "Why didn't you call me?"

"Didn't have a chance. Don't worry about it. You need your lunch, too."

"I was daydreaming. I just went right off."

"It's that sort of a day." Miss Harriet reached across Edie to take a birthday card from a cus-

138

tomer. When the customers had all been waited on and sent back out into the rain, Miss Harriet said, "You did miss one bright spot, during your lunch. Virginia and Crystal were in. I was too busy to go wait on them, so they just stood around for a minute and left in a huff."

"Oh, but did Virginia see your shirt?"

Miss Harriet struggled to hold back a smile. "She gave me her what's-an-old-lady-like-you-doing-in-a-T-shirt look. But Crystal laughed. I think Crystal's brighter than she pretends to be."

"Oh, my gosh! Crystal! Did you check the band?"

"Didn't give it a thought, I'm afraid."

Edie rushed into the other room and checked the high shelf above the boxes of Christmas lights where she had moved the little band. "Well, today she got the accordionist. Darn her!"

"Mark it down some more," Miss Harriet said. "I ought to add the whole set to their charge, that's what I ought to do." She went into her office, sat in front of her typewriter, and stared at the keyboard. "I can't seem to get anything accomplished today," she said.

"It's the weather," Edie said. *And old memories*, she thought.

Edie was just starting for the basement to

get some orders ready for mailing when the phone rang. "Book Bayou," she said. "May I help you?"

"Is this Edie Edmunds?" The gruff voice on the other end of the line sounded familiar. "I need to talk to Harriet."

Mr. Hartwick! "Are you home from the hospital already?" Edie asked.

"They won't let me leave," Mr. Hartwick said. "Harriet not around?"

"She's right here. I'll go get her. Don't hang up."

Edie ran to Miss Harriet's office. "Important call for you," she said. "Hurry!"

"You look like a skunk in a henhouse," Miss Harriet said as she reached for the extension over her desk. "Who is it?"

"Pick it up! You'll see."

Miss Harriet pushed a button and picked up the phone. She listened, and then she gave Edie an amused glance and reached for a pencil.

Edie streaked to the basement, raced through her wrapping, and hurried back upstairs, lugging the canvas mailbag. Miss Harriet was on her knees on the carpet, rummaging through the cabinet where she kept her stock of first editions and rare books that were out of print. She sat back on her heels and grinned

140

up at Edie. "Don't look so smug," she said. "He only wanted to see if I could come up with a few old books he wants to read again."

"Have you got them?"

"Three out of four so far."

"Will you take them over to the hospital tonight?" Edie asked.

"Of course I will. You don't expect his doctors to let him wander down here and collect them, do you? It's just good business, that's all it is."

"Sure, Miss Harriet," Edie said. "That's all it is." She put on her slicker and picked up the mailbag. "You could take them over as soon as I get back from the post office. You could even stay and have dinner in his room with him."

"He'll just have to wait till I get my store closed for the night," Miss Harriet said. "Wouldn't want him to get any ideas."

"Oh, of course not," Edie said. "Well, I'll be back as fast as I can. In case you change your mind." She walked out into the drizzling rain, planning Miss Harriet's wedding all the way to the post office. She hoped it wasn't going to be impossible to find a wedding dress that came in some shade of green or brown.

Chapter Thirteen

On Saturday night Edie hung back at Doctor Paul's front door and let her family go in ahead of her. Michael was cleaned up, for once, and Becky had washed her hair. Edie had hurried home from work with her father, changed into her yellow sundress, and carefully applied some makeup. And then Kate had appeared. She looked like a fashion model. She had blown her hair back from her face in soft waves, and she had put on her good white pants and a plaid shirt that looked brand new. *Why tonight? Who was she trying to impress?*

Edie stopped wondering and looked around Doctor Paul's living room. The walls blazed with

143

the brilliant modern paintings his wife had collected before her death. Edie grinned at Jake
and handed over the Jell-O mold pan. "This is
supposed to be a Spanish cream," she said. "I
made it last night at Julie's house. It's bound
to be terrible."

Becky appeared in the doorway between the
living room and the kitchen, fiddling with a
paper flower in her hair. "I put the stuff that
goes in the middle of Edie's dessert in your
refrigerator," she said, hanging onto Jake's arm.
"It's crunched peanut brittle and whipped
cream."

"I hope I can get the custard unmolded
right," Edie said. "There's caramel on the bottom, and I'm afraid it'll all stay in the pan when
I turn it upside down."

"Never fear," Jake said. "I'm a whiz at
unmolding. Let's put this in the kitchen."

He took a bright yellow paper flower out of
a basket on the counter. He waved the flower in
front of Edie's nose and stood back, hands
propped on his hips, studying her. "Left ear
means you're available, you know," he said. "And
right ear means you're taken. I can't decide
where to put your flower. Are you taken or not,
Edie?"

"Taken by what?" Edie tried to make her

voice sound just as teasing as Jake's had sounded.

"Oh, Jake!" Becky giggled. "You know Edie is left ear. You said all unmarried girls are left ear. You said Mom was the only one who could wear a flower behind her right ear."

"What would I do without you, Beck? You've got a terrific memory for a little kid." Jake fumbled with the hairpin attached to the flower and gently stuck it in Edie's hair over her left ear. It matched her dress perfectly and complemented her golden hair.

"Thanks," Edie said, pushing the flower more securely into place. "I guess this means I am now officially available."

Jake lunged at Edie and growled, "Now I can make you mine forever!"

"How you two carry on," Becky said.

Jake took a crystal pitcher out of the refrigerator and handed it to Becky. "Here, Beck, carry in the sangria for me, will you?"

She took it carefully with both hands. "Don't look so worried, Edie. I'm going to walk real slow. Hey, Jake, did you know there's fruit floating around in this?"

"I noticed that," Jake said. He opened the oven and took out a pan of nachos. "I just have to cut these up a little," he said. "Why don't you go on in the den and tell Uncle Paul happy birthday? There are cold sodas behind the bar in there."

"Let me know if you want any help," Edie said.

Jake smiled at her across the kitchen. "Everything's almost ready. Besides, you already came up with a surprise dessert."

"Better wait till you taste that Spanish cream before you get too excited." Edie picked up Doctor Paul's present and went on to the den.

Doctor Paul was talking with Mr. and Mrs. Edmunds. He waved as Edie came in. Oscar jumped off the back of the couch and came over to rub himself against Edie's ankles. Edie stooped to scratch his head.

"Aren't these two of the biggest cats you've ever seen?" Kate said. "George climbed into my lap the minute I sat down. I'm afraid to move." George was sprawled across Kate's legs, his gray head wedged into the crack between Kate and the arm of the couch.

"I'll get you some sangria," Edie said. She dropped Doctor Paul's present on the table and leaned over to kiss his cheek. "I hope you like it." She poured sangria for Kate, took a Coke for herself, and carried the drinks to the couch.

Doctor Paul unwrapped the book and threw

146

the wrappings on the floor for Oscar to play with. "Great! I've been wanting to read this. Thank you." He handed the book to Mrs. Edmunds. "And I got a basketful of pickles and jelly, too. Such a production for a guy pushing forty."

"Thirty-five is pushing forty?" Mrs. Edmunds said. "Hardly."

"It's too old for a piñata, I think," Becky said. "And Jake's got one hanging in the dining room."

"I'll let you break it by yourself then," Doctor Paul said. "I'm sure going to miss Jake this fall. I suppose I'll have to start advertising for some help soon."

Edie saw his glance flicker over to Kate, but he didn't say anything else.

"You ought to apply for the job," Edie whispered to Kate. "It'd be fun, and you'd never have to work downtown again."

Kate blushed. "I couldn't do that!"

"Well, I don't see why not."

Before Kate could answer, Jake entered the room holding out a tray of nachos.

Kate placed one carefully on her cocktail napkin. "Are the peppers on these hot?" she asked.

147

"No, they're mild," Jake said. "It's safe to take another."

Kate shook her head, but Edie helped herself to three.

Jake offered his tray to Becky, who was trailing a ribbon along the floor for Oscar. She sat up and peered at the nachos. "I don't think I like Mexican cheese," she said.

"It's cheese from Wisconsin," Jake said, "melted on good old American Doritos."

"There's still those green things," Becky said.

"Well, here, I'll take one off for you. C'mon, try this."

Becky took the nacho and nibbled on one corner. "Hey, it's good!"

"Then you can finish passing them, OK?"

Becky took the tray from Jake and carried it over to Doctor Paul.

Jake sat down on the couch between Edie and Kate, but he leaned forward and chatted with Michael across the room. Michael was talking excitedly about some Clint Eastwood movie he'd just seen, and Edie wasn't particularly interested. Still, just sitting next to Jake was nice.

When the sangria and the nachos were gone, Jake ushered everyone into the dining room. Doctor Paul pulled out Kate's chair for her, and Jake pulled out the one for Mrs. Edmunds, then ran around the table to pull out Edie's. He sat down directly across from her. A lazy Susan in front of him was loaded with plates of shredded lettuce, tomatoes, grated cheese, guacamole, and sour cream. A crock pot full of chili bubbled by his right hand. Jake made tostados for everyone, and Edie caught him watching her as she took her first bite. "Like it?" he asked.

"Mmm. Another hit." Edie felt her face flush as he winked at her. "Go on and try yours, Becky," Edie said. "It won't bite."

Becky gingerly scraped off the cheese and the lettuce and the tomatoes and the guacamole and bit into the chili underneath. "Delicious," she proclaimed.

Everybody stuffed themselves with seconds on the tostados, and just when they thought they would burst, Jake carried in Doctor Paul's birthday cake. It showed a man in a white coat, an outsize hypodermic needle in his hand, chasing a herd of cows off the edge of the cake. Two cats, one in orange frosting and the other gray, sat on the top rail of a fence, laughing to each other.

"This is too magnificent to cut," Doctor Paul protested.

"But you're going to, anyway, aren't you?" Becky said.

"I took some pictures of it in the kitchen," Jake said, slicing carefully around the orange cat. He scooped ice cream onto the first plate and handed it to Becky.

"A whole cat! Thanks, Jake!"

Edie's Spanish cream, perfectly unmolded, its golden brown caramel streaking the top of the custard, was passed around the table. "Kate, you must have made this," Doctor Paul said, lathering his helping with whipped cream.

"Not me," Kate said. "Edie came up with that. Though how she managed it with her nose always in a book, I don't know."

"It was a cookbook," Edie said. "That's how."

"Well, it's delicious," Doctor Paul said.

Jake winked at Edie again. "It really is," he said. "We ought to go into business. We could cater parties together."

"Get serious," Edie said. "This is my one and only dish!"

It was late by the time dessert was over. But Jake insisted that everyone make a try at breaking the piñata. He brought out a broomstick and a handkerchief to use as a blindfold. Each guest had to try and hit the piñata while

150

blindfolded. There was much laughter, as one after another, they swung at the air. Becky was given three chances, and on the third she broke it. To her delight candy rained down on the group.

Then Mrs. Edmunds and Kate helped clear the table, and soon all the Edmundses but Edie left for home. She was staying to help clean up.

Doctor Paul started to sweep up the scraps of papier-mâché from the broken piñata, but Jake shoved him out of the way. "Go read your new book," he said. "Enjoy what's left of your big day."

"Remind me, Jake," Doctor Paul said, "that I owe you one heck of a birthday party in October."

"October what?" Edie asked. Maybe she would send him the turkey shirt for his birthday.

"The fourteenth," Jake said. "When's yours?"

"September twenty-third," Edie said.

"You're a Virgo. I always get along with Virgos."

Edie looked out the kitchen window over the sink. "It sure is dark out tonight. Except for that funny streak of light. See? There in the north?"

Jake brushed against Edie's shoulder as he looked out. Suddenly he tossed his dish towel down and grabbed her arm. "C'mon outside! Maybe it's a spaceship!"

Edie saw the arc of light brighten and begin to move, sliding up the sky. "Oh, it's an aurora! I haven't seen one since I was little." She dried her hands and rushed outside behind Jake.

They sat on a picnic bench on the deck and watched the arc move to the zenith of the sky, growing brighter as it went. "I've never seen northern lights," Jake said. "Will they last long, or is this it?"

"It depends. Sometimes there's lots more. I did a paper on auroras last year."

Jake rushed into the house and came out with a blanket. He wrapped it halfway around himself and then pulled Edie close to him to wrap it around her, too. "There," he said. "Snug as bugs."

Edie took a deep breath and gingerly leaned back against Jake's shoulder. Under the blanket, Jake found her hand and held it. The arc was fading. *Don't end yet,* Edie begged the sky. *Oh, don't be over so soon.*

As the arc disappeared, a curtain of pale purple light shot out of nowhere to drip down from the zenith.

"And this is all just supposed to be atmospheric disturbance?" Jake asked. "Hard to believe."

"The Eskimos thought the lights were torches held by the souls of the dead to guide them to a land of happiness."

The curtain began to pulsate as the purple faded into white and then brightened to purple again. Edie couldn't tell how long the pulsation lasted. She felt so warm and comfortable as she leaned on Jake. She let the beauty of the northern lights swoop her up into the sky.

"I was watching you tonight," Jake said. "I like the way you do everything."

"You do?"

"Yeah. You're always so aware of everyone, I guess. You've got this incredible sense of people."

"I like the way you do everything, too," Edie said. "I especially like the way you cook."

Jake laughed and turned his head to kiss her on the nose. The curtain of light in the sky suddenly broke up into shooting rays that zoomed off toward the zenith, turning a brilliant red as they climbed.

"It looks like war, doesn't it?" Jake said. "Only beautiful."

"The Gaels thought the flaming aurora really was a battle in the sky. The red was supposed to be the blood of their gods. People who live way up north say the aurora makes a noise, too, like the sounds of battle."

"It looks like it should. But I don't hear anything."

"Me, neither."

They sat in silence for an hour, watching the light shoot across the black sky. As the rays began to fade and slowly disappear, Jake shifted his arm a little and pulled slightly away from her.

"Your arm must be asleep," she said.

"I'm not complaining, am I?" Jake grinned. "I'm glad you stayed tonight. This was a thing nobody should see alone."

"*Keoeeit*," Edie said. "That was the Eskimo name for the lights."

"I'm going to have to start reading more to keep up with you," Jake said. He stood up and let the blanket fall from his shoulders. The red towers of light were gone, and there was only the faint arc of light again, hanging back in its starting place in the northern sky. "I guess that was the finale." Jake pulled Edie to her feet, bundling the blanket around her.

He took her face between his hands and very slowly leaned toward her, his mouth lightly brushing hers. He drew her close and kissed her. Then he pulled back a bit so he could look

154

into her eyes. "No matter how old I get," he said, "I'll never forget watching northern lights with you. Never."

"Neither will I," Edie said. "With you, I mean."

Jake looped an arm around her shoulders and steered her toward the kitchen. Edie was suddenly in tears, from the kiss, from the aurora, from the wonderful combination. She went straight for the bathroom before Jake could question her wet cheeks.

When she came out, she found Jake waiting for her. His eyes were shining with such a special light that Edie almost turned around to see whom he was looking at. She stopped herself just in time. The light was for her.

When the kitchen was clean and the dishwasher humming, Jake took Edie home. On the Edmundses' front porch, Jake drew her away from the glare of the porchlight and the fluttering moths, and kissed her softly on her forehead, then on each cheek, and then on her nose. This time Edie put her arms around his neck and let her fingers touch his hair.

"You'd better go in before your mother notices you're still out," Jake whispered. He gave her a final kiss on the mouth.

Edie floated into the house. All night long,

she listened to the frogs' concert coming up from the creek. Every time she closed her eyes all she could see was Jake's profile, etched against a sky full of flaming color.

Chapter Fourteen

Edie finally dozed off just before dawn. When the smell of frying bacon woke her a little later, she stretched out her legs, testing for weariness, and was surprised to find she didn't feel too bad.

She got out of bed and took her paycheck envelope out of her handbag. With the excitement of the party the night before, she had forgotten to open it. She pulled out the check and stared at it. Miss Harriet had made a big mistake. The check was written for twenty-five dollars too much. Edie slipped the check, unsigned, into her handbag. She would tell Miss Harriet about it first thing.

Downstairs, Mr. Edmunds was cooking

bacon on the big electric griddle. "We'll just about make that next payment," he was saying as Edie came into the kitchen. "As long as none of the herd goes dry this week."

"Don't borrow trouble," Mrs. Edmunds said, whipping the eggs in the yellow bowl. "That bacon's almost ready. Edie, are your sisters up yet?"

"Kate's in the bathroom, but Becky's still dead to the world. Where's Michael?"

"Still milking the cows," Mr. Edmunds said.

"Daddy, if you need money this week, I could help some. I've saved almost all of my paychecks so far."

Mr. Edmunds shook the bacon tongs at her. "That's your college money. We'll make it just fine."

Edie shrugged. "OK, but you know what? Miss Harriet overpaid me twenty-five dollars yesterday. It's incredible how absentminded she's become since Mr. Hartwick got sick."

"Maybe she's giving you a raise," Mrs. Edmunds said. "Listen, go rouse Becky, would you? And then come start the toast. Michael will be in from the barn any minute."

"Not that much of a raise! Would she? Without telling me?" Edie went back upstairs, her head whirling with figures.

She pulled off Becky's blankets, making her groan. "Get up, sleepiness," Edie said. "Or you're going to miss Dad's Sunday special."

Becky sat up, leaning back on her elbows. "I can't do that. Not after my stomach grumbled all night. It was a good thing I liked the nachos and the cake, or I might've starved to death." Becky ducked under her bed to find her robe and struggled into it. "Did you and Jake dance after we left? Did you dance till dawn?"

"Dance? We didn't dance. I was home by midnight. Did you get to see the northern lights?"

"I knew I shouldn't have gone to bed. I had a feeling I was going to miss something big. Were they as good as the pictures in the books?"

"Even better," Edie said. "Don't worry, they'll come again."

"Probably when I'm a hundred. I never get to do anything. You get to go on picnics in the woods. You get to stay late and help clean up parties. What do I ever get to do?"

"Quit your griping," Edie said. "Jake said maybe we'd all go to the beach later today. You're invited, too."

"That's more like it!" Becky said. "Let's go eat."

* * *

Edie clutched the phone between her shoulder and her ear and listened to Jake. "I think I'll just sack out on the sand," he said. "I didn't sleep much last night."

"Neither did I. Too much excitement, I guess."

"You complaining? I wasn't!"

"Oh, no, Jake! Last night was the best. I wouldn't trade it for all the sleep in the world." Edie snuck a glance at her mother, who was taking in Edie's end of the conversation with an amused smile on her face.

"I wouldn't trade it, either," Jake said. "Are Kate and Becky beaching it with us, too?"

"Becky's been prancing around in her inner tube since breakfast. Even Kate seems to want to come. I guess she's not afraid she'll run into Steve way up at Good Hart."

"What about Michael? I suppose he has work to do."

"That never ends around here. But we'll have fun without him."

"Sure," Jake said. "I may try to drag Uncle Paul away from his paperwork to come along. Will you all eat BLTs? That's what I'm making."

"Even Becky will. I'll bring the tomatoes. We're loaded with them."

"Great. I'll just finish packing up the cooler

and get Uncle Paul to put on his swimming trunks. Then I'll be over."

Edie hung up and dashed toward the back door. "I'm going out to pick some tomatoes, OK? Jake's making BLTs for everybody. Even Doctor Paul's coming."

Kate dropped the fork she was drying and quickly bent to pick it up. "Maybe I won't go after all," she said. "My hair's a mess."

"Oh, Kate. You already said you'd come. Your hair still looks great from last night."

Mrs. Edmunds patted Kate's shoulder. "Go and enjoy yourself for a change. The wind up there will destroy everybody else's hair as well. Edie, take all the tomatoes you want. Less for me to have to turn into catsup later."

Edie was just tucking the last tomato slice into the plastic bag when Jake pulled into the backyard. Doctor Paul, wearing a straw sombrero, was in the passenger seat. As he jumped out of the jeep, Becky raced outside with a whoop and took his seat.

Doctor Paul went over to the steps and took the pile of beach towels Kate was carrying. Edie stowed the bag of tomatoes in the cooler. "We'll sit in back with the picnic," Jake said, "and let Uncle Paul drive, since he can find Good Hart and I can't."

"Becky, come back here with us," Edie said, and as Becky climbed over, Kate slid into the front seat. Doctor Paul grinned at her as he got in behind the wheel.

"About time you took a day off," he said.

"About time for the busy country doctor to have a day off, too," Kate said. She was grinning right back at Doctor Paul. Edie saw a flush creep up her cheeks.

She glanced at Jake. Did he see what was going on in the front seat? Jake was busy trying to fit the cooler onto the floor so he could sit closer to Edie. *I wonder,* thought Edie. *How long have they had a thing for each other? Doctor Paul's fifteen years older than Kate. Is that too old? And Kate said just last night she couldn't ever work for him! That should've been my first clue!*

"What are you grinning about?" Jake said.

"I'm not sure. It's just such a perfect beach day, I guess. Isn't that reason enough?" Edie tightened the scarf around her head and settled back against Jake's shoulder to enjoy the winding ride around the bay to the hills north of Harbor Springs.

A wooden arrow pointed the way to the beach through the old Indian cemetery next to the little white church. The graves were marked by white crosses and bunches of flowers.

"You're positive Lake Michigan's someplace in here?" Jake said.

"Keep walking," Edie said. "But stay on the path. There's poison ivy all over the place."

"I bet it won't be too crowded," Doctor Paul said. "I only saw half a dozen cars back there along the road."

"I can't believe half a dozen people could locate this place," Jake said. "I've never been on such a curvy road in all my life."

"When it's the only part of the shoreline not privately owned," Edie said, "people can find it. It's the most gorgeous place in the world."

They heard the crash of waves before they were out of the woods. Jake handed the cooler down the steep bank of a washout to Doctor Paul, then reached back for Edie's arm. Edie shook off his hand and jumped, landing on her hands and knees in the sand, past a tangle of dead brush. "Should've known you'd have your own method," Jake said, jumping after her.

The waves were furiously battering the beach as Edie ran through the tall grass after Becky. A few groups of people were strung out along the sand, each group nestled against its own sand dune. Jake led the way far down the beach and spread out a blanket.

"I can't wait to try those waves," Doctor Paul said. "I see Becky's already beat me to it. I can't remember the last time I was here. You coming in, Kate?"

Kate pulled her sweatshirt over her head and ran behind Doctor Paul to the water, where Becky was crashing into shore in her inner tube. "It's freezing!" Becky shrieked. "It's wonderful. Hurry up!"

"I think I'll just watch the clouds go by," Jake said to Edie. "If you'll keep me company."

"You bet I'm going to. Kate'll watch Becky." Edie lay on her stomach next to Jake and propped herself on her elbows. "It's so peaceful here I never want to leave. That's the only trouble with this beach."

"People talk about northern Michigan magic," Jake said. "This place is sure part of it. I'm going to hate to go back downstate."

"At least East Lansing's not all the way downstate. You can always come up for a weekend. I mean, if you want to."

Jake playfully pulled a strand of Edie's wavy hair. "Only if you'll teach me how to build a snowman," he said, laughing.

"Wait'll you see how much snow we get!"

"Of course, I figure by wintertime you'll have other guys hanging off each arm."

"Who, me? Not a chance."

"At least you could save me the weekends."

Edie shaded her eyes with one hand. "I don't think there'll be a problem," she said. "But I'll save them anyway."

Jake's face was very serious as he bent over and kissed her. "Keeping an eye on you long-distance isn't going to be easy," he said.

Edie touched his face gently. "Really! There's nobody around here I care about."

"We'll see," Jake said. His face was cheerful again as he pulled her to her feet. "Kate seems to be having a great time, doesn't she? Let's go get wet."

Edie edged into the icy water of Lake Michigan, which never really warmed up this far north. "Have you noticed it's Doctor Paul she seems to be enjoying?"

Jake stopped splashing water on his shoulders and stared at Kate body-surfing between Doctor Paul and Becky. "Hey, you know, that wouldn't be a bad combination! But I never dreamed, did you?"

"Not till today," Edie said. She grinned at Jake and dove into the center of a green wave just before it hit her. Jake followed and came up sputtering. They rode the waves till they were blue with cold, and then everyone raced back to the beach for towels and sandwiches.

After lunch Becky went to the water's edge to toss bread crusts to the swooping seagulls. Kate and Doctor Paul stretched out next to each other and dozed in the sun. And Edie and Jake took a long walk down the beach.

"I wish today could last forever." Edie sighed.

Jake answered her with a kiss.

On the way home Edie sat lazily with her head resting on Jake's sunburned shoulder. Once she saw Doctor Paul's hand come down to cover Kate's. He pulled it back as if it had been an accident, but Kate smiled up at him. *You really don't need words*, thought Edie, *just little touches. Little zings.*

Jake had his arm around Edie. He smelled like clean sheets dried in the sun. And the curly red hair on his chest tickled her nose when he pulled her close for a fast hug.

Edie was happier than she had ever been. If only the green, leafy, wonderful fullness of summer weren't passing so quickly. But soon she would be planning her first winter weekend with Jake. He could borrow her father's cross-country skis, and they could have a picnic in the snow—hot chocolate, marshmallows, and all. Maybe she could even figure out how to make her mom's good bean soup by then. And she would have Jake to keep her warm.

Chapter Fifteen

Miss Harriet was wearing a new kelly-green dress when Edie came into Book Bayou on Monday. "That's a wonderful color," Edie said. "You ought to wear more of it."

"Every now and again, I get a little sick of avocado myself. You look as if you got some sun yesterday."

"We went up to Good Hart. It was a gorgeous day." Edie took her paycheck out of her handbag. "Miss Harriet, I wanted to show you something. You paid me too much last week."

Miss Harriet waved the check away. "Nope. It was time you had a raise," she said. "I couldn't do without you, you know."

"But this much more?"

"Definitely. You don't need to look so worried. I'm loaded. Didn't anybody ever tell you that?"

"Well, no, nobody did. But thank you. I'm going to need a lot of money if I can't get a full scholarship for college."

Miss Harriet pointed at the check in Edie's hand. "Lots more where that came from if you can't. You'd be a good investment."

"My dad would never let you help that way. I just know he wouldn't hear of it."

"Well, we've got two more years of high school to get him to see the light," Miss Harriet said. "You leave your dad to me."

"But I just couldn't let you spend all that money on . . ."

"I'll spend it where I please," Miss Harriet said. "Not another word about it for now. We've got a store that needs opening."

Edie got out a broom, wishing she were alone to do a little dance with it. Her father would never let Miss Harriet give her all that money. But maybe if it were a loan? If she promised to pay her back? It would be wonderful not to have to worry about money for a change.

Edie was putting out new birthday cards when Miss Harriet emerged from her office. "Did Mr. Hartwick tell you he's getting out of the hospital on Sunday?" Edie asked. "Mom's throwing a surprise hamburger-and-corn-on-the-cob party for him to celebrate. Dad's picking him up. You will come, won't you?"

"I'd have to check my calendar. I have a feeling I've got something else on for Sunday."

"Oh, you do not, Miss Harriet! And unless you're there, Mr. Hartwick won't put up with the party for more than a minute. You've got to come."

"I ought to come just to start getting to know your mom and dad better, I suppose. Is your young man going to be there?"

"Yes, and Doctor Paul, too."

"I'll supply the dessert," Miss Harriet said promptly. "Gus always did favor Jesperson's lemon meringue pies." She stopped suddenly and looked hard at Edie. "Not that a man's tastes can't change over forty-five years, of course."

"I bet nothing's changed, Miss Harriet. You'll see. So don't worry."

Miss Harriet glanced toward the front of the store as the door opened. "Fiddlesticks!"

she muttered. Virginia and Crystal Lamoreaux marched in.

"We came early today, Harriet," Virginia said. "Since you were too busy to wait on us last time. I need a copy of *The Prophet* for a wedding tomorrow."

"I'll get one wrapped up for you right away," Miss Harriet said. "Your special order finally came in."

Edie crossed the store to guard the remains of the band from Crystal.

"Let the girl do it," Virginia said. "I like her wrapping better than yours. You may show me the Christmas card books. You know what I like."

Edie hated to leave Crystal alone, but she had no choice. She went behind the counter and opened a package of wedding gift-wrap. Miss Harriet was standing over Virginia, who was seated in one of the easy chairs. "You take that dust jacket off right now, miss!" Virginia ordered. "I'm watching you."

Sheepishly, Edie took off the cover. "I'm sorry. I can't believe I'd forget."

Crystal came out of the other room and leaned over the counter, whispering to Edie, "That's the best trick in the world! It is a trick, isn't it? With the dust jackets?"

Edie looked up at Crystal's happy face and tried hard not to laugh.

"I knew it!" Crystal whispered. "I can see it in your eyes. But don't worry, I'll never tell *her*!"

Crystal sauntered casually over to the paperback table. She picked up the new romance Edie had chosen especially for its lurid cover, just in the hopes of irritating Virginia.

"Come here, Crystal!" Virginia commanded. "Tell me if you like this card."

Crystal, already nodding her head, hurried to the fireplace. Edie finished wrapping the gift while Miss Harriet wrote up the card order. The next second, Jeremy the chauffeur rapped on the front window, and the Lamoreaux sisters whisked themselves out to their car.

Edie ran into the other room to check the band. "Miss Harriet, look at this! Crystal's put every piece back!"

Miss Harriet snickered. "Well. Mark the darn thing back up! I wonder why she had a change of heart?"

"I think it was our trick on Virginia with the dust jackets," Edie said. "Crystal told me she loved it. That's what we were whispering about."

"I give up," said Miss Harriet. "I can't wait till Labor Day gets here and they go home to Baton Rouge."

The phone rang, and Edie went to the counter to answer it.

"It's only your friendly neighborhood lobster," Jake said. "Want to have lunch today around one? We could grab a fast pizza."

"I'd love it. I can't wait to see your sunburn." Edie told Jake goodbye and picked up the feather duster. Everything needed a good dusting.

"Miss Harriet? Have you actually sold one of those really awful romances I bought to make Virginia mad?"

"Nope," Miss Harriet said. "They're both still there."

Edie giggled. "No, they're not. Only one is. And I saw Crystal looking at them before! I'll bet she swiped one."

"Good for Crystal!" Miss Harriet said. "I can just see her reading it under her bedcovers by flashlight."

Edie laughed. "That's the best trick on Virginia yet. I'm glad Crystal thought up one of her own. She'll probably bring the book back next week. By the way, that was Jake on the phone before. He wants to buy me lunch, around one if it's OK."

"I'll eat now, then. Remind me to order the pies for Sunday."

"Order the pies for Sunday," Edie said, as Miss Harriet started her daily search for the purse on the cluttered counter. "Couldn't I just weed out a few of these out-of-date catalogs while you're gone?"

"Better not," Miss Harriet said. "I'm sure I'll need them tomorrow if you do." Miss Harriet headed across the street for her grilled cheese, and Edie went back to work on the card racks.

"Ooh, you look like you're in pain," Edie said as Jake opened the door of the pizza place.

Jake grinned. "Only hurts when I laugh. Uncle Paul gave me some good lotion. I'll have a tan by tomorrow."

"You hope. Let's have pepperoni."

"OK. In fact, let's have everything but anchovies. And maybe no onions. In case you're planning on a kiss after we eat."

"I could manage that," Edie said.

"We want a large pizza," Jake said to the

boy behind the order desk. "No anchovies, no onions, but everything else."

When the pizza was ready, Jake carried the hot pan around the bank of electronic games to the dark cave of a room filled with tables and booths. Edie started as she noticed Sean and Liza eating meatball sandwiches in the first booth. Liza glanced at Jake as he went past and smiled falsely at Edie. Sean was too busy eating to look up. He had meat sauce on his chin.

Edie sat across from Jake and lifted her first piece of pizza from the pan. Three pieces later, she realized she was actually relaxed, eating in the same room with Sean. He really didn't matter anymore.

As Sean and Liza got up to leave, Sean looked over at Edie and flipped her a wave. Edie flipped the wave back and leaned across the booth to kiss Jake. She laughed at his look of surprise. "I thought we were going to wait till we were done," he said.

"I just couldn't wait a minute longer," Edie said.

On Sunday Edie was husking corn over the barnyard gate when Jake and Doctor Paul drove up. Two cows crowded each other on the far side of the fence, lipping up the corn husks. Jake jogged down the hill toward her. "I thought we'd be late. Isn't Miss Harriet here yet?"

"She was here once already. But she left the pies at home and had to go all the way back to town. I hope she gets back before Dad and Mr. Hartwick arrive."

Jake fed the last husks to the cows and picked up Edie's basket. "I'm going to eat at least twelve of these. Is the fire all set?"

"Yup. Kate's ready to put the hamburgers on as soon as everybody shows up. You can help me wrap the corn in foil."

When they finished wrapping the corn, they carried it to the grill where Kate was laughing at the frilly apron Doctor Paul had tied around his waist. Mrs. Edmunds came out of the house carrying a tray loaded with hamburger fixings just as Miss Harriet's car bounced up the driveway. Edie ran to greet her.

She was wearing the kelly-green dress again and had even put some blusher on her cheeks. "Did I beat him back? I went as fast as the law allows."

"You're fine. Come say hello to Mom."

Mrs. Edmunds set the lemon pies on the

picnic table and shook Miss Harriet's hand. "I can't tell you how Edie raves about you," she said. "She's having a grand summer."

"And so am I," Miss Harriet said, smiling at Edie.

"Here they come!" Kate shouted as the pickup turned in off the road. "Michael, come on! Everybody be ready. On the count of three."

Mr. Hartwick stepped out of the truck and looked at all the people, a dazed expression on his face. His old blue suit coat hung loosely around him, but his step was firm. He walked without leaning on Mr. Edmunds, who kept a cautious hand at Mr. Hartwick's elbow.

Jake waved his hands three times like a conductor, and everyone screamed, "Welcome home, Mr. Hartwick!"

Mr. Hartwick spread his arms wide. "What's this fuss? You here, too, Harriet? Didn't sell me enough books last week?"

"Don't excite yourself, Gus," Miss Harriet said. "You old fool."

"Bet you thought I'd never walk out of that place on my own steam, didn't you?" Mr. Hartwick said.

"Oh, I knew you would," Miss Harriet said. "Nobody as crabby as you ever dies."

"Well, I like your dress," Mr. Hartwick said. "Brighter than the usual, though."

"I like it that way," Miss Harriet said. "Come, sit down and rest."

"Been resting for two weeks!" But Mr. Hartwick sank into a lawn chair anyway.

Mr. Hartwick turned to Jake. "Never did get to thank you in person, young fellow."

"Well, we're all glad you're back on your feet. How many hamburgers can you eat?"

"One to start with," Mr. Hartwick said.

"Don't stuff yourself," Miss Harriet said. "I brought lemon pies from Jesperson's for dessert."

"Lemon pies?" Mr. Hartwick's frail smile twitched a little at one corner. "Lemon pies. Well, I'll be." He stared at Miss Harriet from under his bushy eyebrows till she looked away.

Jake came up behind Edie and wrapped his arms around her waist. "We'll never know their whole story, I guess. Do you suppose we'll ever be such a mystery to anybody?"

"We might," Edie said. "But I'd rather not be." She brushed one finger lightly over Jake's peeling nose and grinned up at him. "Would you?"

"Not me," Jake said, rocking her gently from side to side.

"Ee-yew!" shouted Becky. "Look at Jake and Edie. They're really—"

"Becky!" Kate called. "I'm ready for the buns."

Becky darted up the porch steps and was back in a moment, the buns clutched under one arm and her chrysalis jar in her hands. "Doctor Paul, quick! My butterfly's finished, I think. Come see if he's all right."

Becky shook the butterfly out onto the mock orange bush. It clung to a leaf, opening and closing its orange and black wings. "He's just drying off," Doctor Paul said. "Let him sit a-while." Doctor Paul took the buns and went back to help Kate.

Mr. Hartwick laughed at Becky hovering over the butterfly and took a deep breath of fresh country air. "Been gone a long time. Indeed I have. It's good to be back."

"And it's good to have you back, Gus," Miss Harriet said. "I'll go fix you a plate." Edie saw the glint of tears in Miss Harriet's eyes as she walked over to the grill.

Edie waited till all the others had served themselves before she assembled her own plate. Then she carried her food to the picnic table where Jake was just starting his second ear of corn. Jake elbowed Michael in the ribs as she came up behind him. "Make room for my girl there," he said cheerfully.

Edie stepped over the bench, balancing herself with one hand on Jake's shoulder. It was wonderful to have her own special shoulder to lean on. She touched Jake's arm and pointed across the yard. The butterfly had left the mock orange bush and was wobbling through the air toward the magnolia tree.

"That guy picked a perfect day to hatch, didn't he?" Jake said.

"The very best," Edie said.

The lights in Jake's dark eyes were blazing. "The best so far, you mean."

"A better day than this?" Edie said. "There couldn't be."

Jake gave her a squeeze. "Let's wait and see," he said.

Edie pulled on one of his curls and let it spring back into place. "I'll have to keep my eyes peeled then, I guess," she said. "We have a few more days of summer left."

"I don't have to leave till September first," Jake said. "Let's drink to the rest of the summer." He solemnly raised his glass of iced tea.

Edie raised her glass of lemonade just as solemnly and took a sip.

Jake's arm tightened around her waist, and he reached for the corn platter with his free hand. Edie looked around the table to make sure everyone was busy eating, then she leaned over and kissed Jake softly on his ear.

Read these great new Sweet Dreams romances,
on sale soon!

( ) #33 DEAR AMANDA by Rosemary Vernon (On sale
February 15, 1983 • 23283-5 • $1.95)

Tina is so excited about her mysterious new identity created
by the success of her "Dear Amanda" advice column in the
school paper—and students are really taking her advice! But
something is still missing from her life—that special feeling
for one particular boy. How can she be so unhappy when
things are going so well? And why are other people's problems
so much easier to solve than her own?

( ) #34 COUNTRY GIRL by Melinda Pollowitz (On sale
February 15, 1983 • 23287-8 • $1.95)

When Sean suddenly drops Edie for another girl, Edie thinks
she'll never be able to forget hm. Then she meets Jake. Fun-
loving and caring, he makes Edie feel warm and happy inside.
They spend long, happy days laughing together and taking
quiet walks in the country. Part of Edie is sure that Jake is
the boy for her, but after losing Sean, she's awfully frightened.
Can she learn to give her heart again?

( ) #35 FORBIDDEN LOVE by Marian Woodruff (On sale
March 15, 1983 • 23338-6 • $1.95)

Although backing into Tim's car in the school parking lot
wasn't the kind of first impression Patti had wanted to make,
the accident turns out to be the beginning of a wonderful
relationship—until their parents start arguing. Patti and Tim
continue to see each other secretly, but they hate sneaking
around. When will their parents stop acting like children,
and listen to reason?

( ) #36 SUMMER DREAMS by Barbara Conklin (On sale March 15, 1983 • 23339-4 • $1.95)

Katy's summer looks to be the most rewarding one of her life—she'll be helping Michael, a little blind boy, get over a recent tragedy, and Steve Kaplan, the boy of her dreams, will be working with her. But as the summer draws to a close Michael is turning out to be more than she can handle—and Steve, though friendly, remains distant. When they say good-bye to Michael, will Katy and Steve be losing each other, too?

( ) THE BODY BOOK by Julie Davis (On sale March 15, 1983 • 23376-5 • $1.95)

Are you happy with the shape you're in? Chances are you'd like to lose five pounds, firm up your tummy, round out your figure, or strengthen your legs. Well, you're not alone—everyone can use some improvement, and by using THE BODY BOOK'S easy-to-follow program of exercise and nutrition, *you* can decide just how healthy and attractive you'll be.

Buy these books at your local bookstore or use this handy coupon for ordering:

This February, the battle
between Good and Evil begins in earnest . . .

DARK FORCES

INTRODUCING AN EXCITING NEW OCCULT SERIES FOR TEENS!

DARK FORCES books blend supernatural suspense into the familiar world of high school—romance, cars, and pizza. The first four titles go on sale February 9th.

☐ #1—THE GAME by Les Logan (22835-8 • $1.95)

When a car accident places Julie in a wheelchair, she rejects all of her friends to spend hours playing with a Ouija board. Then she becomes possessed by something unspeakable, and only her identical twin, Terri, can rid her of a terrifying, evil demon.

☐ #2—THE MAGIC SHOW by Laurie Bridges and Paul Alexander (22833-1 • $1.95)

A sorcerer's ancient book of spells plunges Chris into an evil world of black magic and demons, a world which can grant him anything—power, money, even love. But a voice from beyond the grave demands one more thing—vengeance—and Chris's girlfriend must stop him from performing a bloody ritual that can only end in death.

☐ #3—THE DOLL by Rex Sparger (22824-2 • $1.95)

When Jack wins his girlfriend, Cassie, a doll for her collection, she can't be happier—until strange and horrifying accidents begin to occur. Then Jack realizes that something has invaded Cassie's very soul, and he must fight to save the girl he loves from the demonic rage of THE DOLL.

☐ #4—DEVIL WIND by Laurie Bridges and

Paul Alexander (22834-X • $1.95)

A quiet afternoon sail around some mysterious coves seemed like the perfect romantic setting to Peter and Mary Anne—until a sudden storm, an antique whistle, and an ancient curse plunged Peter into a terrifying nightmare of witches and warlocks . . . a nightmare that only Mary Anne could wake him from.

Buy these books at your local bookstore or use this handy coupon for ordering